The BLEEDI
of the STO

The BLEEDING *of the* STONE

BY IBRAHIM AL-KONI

translated by May Jayyusi & Christopher Tingley

Interlink Books
An imprint of Interlink Publishing Group, Inc.
New York • Northampton

First published in 2002 by

INTERLINK BOOKS
An imprint of Interlink Publishing Group, Inc.
99 Seventh Avenue • Brooklyn, New York 11215 and
46 Crosby Street • Northampton, Massachusetts 01060
www.interlinkbooks.com

Library of Congress Cataloging-in-Publication Data
Al-Koni, Ibrahim.
  [Nazif al-Úhajar. English]
  The bleeding of the stone / by Ibrahim Al-Koni ; translated by May Jayyusi and Christopher Tingley—
1st English translation.
     p. cm.
  ISBN 1-56656-417-4
  I. Jayyusi, May. II. Tingley, Christopher. III. Title.
  PJ7842.U54 N3913 2002
  892.7'36—dc21

                          2001003664

Printed and bound in Canada by Webcom Ltd.

Cover painting "Unity," 1980, by Sami Burhan,
courtesy of The Royal Society of Fine Arts, Jordan National Gallery of Fine Art,
Amman, Jordan.

This English translation is published with the cooperation of PROTA (the Project of Translation from Arabic); director: Salma K. Jayyusi, Cambridge, Massachusetts, USA.

To request our complete 48-page full-color catalog,
please call us toll free at **1-800-238-LINK,** visit our
website at **www.interlinkbooks.com**, or write to
Interlink Publishing
46 Crosby Street, Northampton, MA 01060
e-mail: info@interlinkbooks.com

ﺳ

1. THE STONE ICON

There are no animals on land or birds flying on their wings, but are communities like your own.

—Quran 6:38

And it came to pass, when they were in the field, that Cain rose up against Abel his brother, and slew him. And the Lord said unto Cain, Where is Abel thy brother? And he said, I know not: Am I my brother's keeper? And He said, What hast thou done? The voice of thy brother's blood crieth unto Me from the ground. And now art thou cursed from the earth, which hath opened her mouth to receive thy brother's blood from thy hand; When thou tillest the ground, it shall not henceforth yield unto thee her strength; a fugitive and a vagabond shalt thou be in the earth.

—Genesis 4:8–12

It was only when he started praying that the male goats decided to butt one another right there in front of him.

Evening was coming, the flaming disk of the sun sinking slowly down from the depths of the sky as it bade farewell, with the threat to return next morning and finish burning what it hadn't burned today, and Asouf plunged his arms into the sands of the wadi to begin his ablutions, in readiness for his afternoon prayers. Hearing the roar of the engine from afar, he decided to hurry and give God His due before the Christians arrived, so as to be ready as usual to welcome them to the wadi and show them the figures painted on the rocks.

But Satan entered the goats, who took evident pleasure in butting at the very moment he said "God is great" and began murmuring the *Fatiha*,[i] as if they were proud of their horns or wanted to show him their skill. They were restless today because a skittish she-goat had led on a headstrong male. He'd been following her since the morning, probing her rear with his nose, trying, incessantly, to climb up on her from behind, and this had aroused the jealousy of the other goats, who'd gathered together and begun the contest, using their horns as weapons.

Cutting short his prayer, he cursed the devil, then went to pray in front of the most prominent rock in the Wadi Matkhandoush. This stood at the end of the wadi's western slope, where it met the Wadi Aynesis to form a single valley, deep and wide, sweeping down northeast until it merged, at last, into the Great Abrahoh in Massak Mallat.

The mighty rock marked the end of a series of caves, standing there like a cornerstone. Through thousands of years it had faced the merciless sun, adorned with the most wondrous paintings ancient man had made anywhere in the Sahara. There was the giant priest depicted over the full height of the rock, hiding his face behind that mysterious mask. His hand touched the *waddan*[ii] that stood there alongside him, its air both dignified and stubborn, its head raised, like the priest's, toward the far horizon where the sun rose to pour its rays each day on their faces.

Through thousands of years the mighty priest and the sacred *waddan* had kept those features, clear and deep, majestic and vivid, set in the heart of the solid rock. There the priest stood, taller and larger than man's natural figure, inclined a little toward the sacred *waddan*. That too surpassed a normal *waddan* in size.

When, as a young man, Asouf had crossed the desolate wadi herding his goats, he'd never dreamed these paintings were so important. Today they'd become a focus for Christian tourists, who came from the most distant countries to see them, crossing the desert in their special desert trucks to gaze at the stone, their mouths open in amazement before its enigmatic splendor and beauty. Once he'd even seen a European woman kneel in front of the rock, murmuring indistinct words, and he'd known instinctively the words were Christian prayers.

Similar paintings adorned mountain rocks and caverns in the other wadis, throughout the Massak Satfat. He'd discovered them when, as a child, he'd tire himself out chasing after his unruly herd and go into the caves to find refuge from the sun, seizing a few moments of rest and amusing himself by gazing at the colored figures: at hunters with long, strange faces pursuing a variety of animals, among which he recognized only the *waddan* and the gazelle and the wild ox. Painted on the rocks, too, were naked women with great breasts, huge indeed, out of all proportion to the size of their bodies. This had made him laugh, as he thought of the breasts getting in the women's way as they walked along! He'd leaned back and shrieked with laughter, the echo ringing strangely through the unknown caves.

Then, as he climbed the mountains behind the goats, he'd discovered still further paintings. He saw, painted on the rock walls, hideous faces like the faces of ghouls, and of ugly animals not found in the desert. How was it his mother had never told him about these, even in her fairy tales? His father had never mentioned them either, before he died in dreadful pursuit of that charmed *waddan*.

"They're the people who used to live in the caves," his mother told him. "The first ancestors."

"But," he objected, "you said jinn lived in the caves."

She gazed at him bemused, then smiled, rocking right and left as she shook the milk in her hands.

"Are our ancestors jinn?" he persisted.

She stifled a laugh, but he saw it in her eyes even so. He repeated his question, and this time she just snapped:

"Ask your father."

And so he asked his father, who laughed outright.

"Perhaps they were from the jinn," he said. "But from the good jinn. The jinn are like people. They're divided into two tribes: the tribe of good and the tribe of evil. We belong to the first tribe—to the jinn who chose good."

"Is that why we don't have any close neighbors?"

"Yes, that's why. If you live near bad people, their evil will strike you. Anyone choosing the good has to flee from people, to make sure no evil comes to him. That's what this group of jinn did. They lived in caves, from time immemorial, away from evil. Can't you hear them talking together, on moonlit nights?"

His mother broke in.

"Why are you frightening him," she said, "with all this stuff about the jinn talking at night? Why don't you go and milk the camel instead, so I can have some milk before supper?"

Laughing again, his father went off. Asouf turned to his mother.

"I hear the jinn in the caves every day," he said. "Talking to one another. They say the strangest things, and they even start singing sometimes. I'm not afraid of the jinn."

She laughed and threw some pieces of wood on the fire.

Asouf still took pleasure in the jinn faces in the mountain caves. Fleeing the scorching heat, he'd take refuge, panting, among the hollows of the rocks. There he'd lie for a time, then crawl to the rocky wall and start taking off the layers of dust, until the lines painted in the rocks would begin to appear. Still he'd go on, wiping away at the mighty walls, until at last the faces would appear, masked or long, or else animals fleeing from the arrows of the masked hunters: *waddan*, gazelles, oxen and many others, huge in size, with long legs he never saw in the desert today.

In time he began calling the wadis and chasms and mountains by the names of the figures painted on their rocks. This was the Wadi of Gazelles, that the Path of the Hunters, that the *Waddan* Mountain, that, again, the Herdsmen's Plain; until, finally, he'd discovered the great jinni, the masked giant rising alongside his dignified *waddan*, his face turned toward the *qibla*,[iii] awaiting sunrise and praising Almighty God in everlasting prayer.

He was chasing the most unruly goats in the herd, who'd strayed from the rest, down the desolate Wadi Matkhandoush. He caught up with them, finally, at the place where the wadi merged with the nearby Aynesis, to form one deep, stately river valley, winding its difficult way across the barren desert, veering toward the Abrahoh plain. There a cluster of caves stood, crowned by mighty rocks; and these were flanked by that one towering rock that stood like a building soaring toward the sky, like a pagan statue fashioned by the gods. The masked jinni, with his sacred *waddan*, covered the colossal stone face from top to bottom. He stood long gazing at the tableau, then tried, vainly, to climb the rocks to touch the great jinni's mask.

There were boulders strewn around the rock face. He tried to gain a hold on the smooth rocks, but some stones gave way under his feet, and he fell on his back into the wadi.

He struggled on for a while, writhing with pain, then crawled on all fours to try and find some shade beneath a tall, green palm tree standing in the middle of the wadi. His heart was beating violently, the sweat trickling from his body. When he reached the tree, the shade had vanished. This surprised him. But he stretched out under the tree even so, waiting for the cruelly beating sun to set.

Next day, he found that the unruly goat, who had wandered from the herd and led him to the cave of the master jinni, had been snatched by a wolf that same night; and he remembered how the palm tree had abandoned him, stealing its shade away, when he'd taken refuge there after falling from the rock.

ر

2. Praying before the Guardian Idol

He finished his prayer and leaned back his head, still
gazing at the vast wall soaring above him. The master
jinni was blessing him. From behind the veil that strange look
expressed contentment and calm. The majestic *waddan*,
crowned with its two curved horns, was in harmony with its
god; the prayer had, it appeared, been accepted, and the
waddan had found favor with the deity of the shrine.

All unwittingly, Asouf had failed to direct his prayer
toward the Ka'aba. Instead, while prostrating himself, he'd
been facing the stone figure towering above his head from the
depths of the wadi.

The roaring of the truck was coming closer. He rose to
gather his scattered goats before the tourists arrived, and
before evening fell. The animals were dispersed, some in the
nearby wadi, while others had climbed the mountain slopes,
looking for grass among the rocks, the males pursuing the
skittish females with tireless energy.

He could, he reckoned, fetch back the stray goats and
gather the herd before the guests arrived, for the sound of the
engine didn't mean the truck was actually that close. Sounds
in the desert could deceive and delude. In early morning, and

in the evening, the calm magnified the remotest noise and brought it nearer, turning it to clamorous din.

He recalled the time, a few years before, when the men from the Archeological Department had come with a whole caravan of trucks. They'd spent the night in Matkhandoush, and with them was an old Italian said to be a great expert; he was tall and slim with white hair, and he'd protected his eyes from the sun with big black glasses, all the while jotting things down in a notebook that never left his hands. All day long he leaped among the rocks, just like the unruly young goats. He was agile and quick-footed, able to climb mountains with an ease and grace you wouldn't have expected in a man of his age.

They'd dined on a young gazelle they'd brought from Massak Mallat. Then, next morning, they'd presented him with some cans of sardine and tuna fish, along with canned milk and a loaf of white bread.

"From now on," the department official told him, "you're the guardian of the Wadi Matkhandoush. You'll be our eyes here. A lot of people will come, from all races and religions, to look at these ancient things. You must watch them. Don't let them steal the stones. See they don't spoil the rocks. These rocks are a great treasure, and these paintings are our country's pride. Keep your eyes open. People are greedy, ready to grab anything. If they can, they'll steal our rocks to sell them in their own country, for thousands, or millions even. Keep your eyes peeled! You're the guardian."

Then, with a weary gesture, he produced ten pounds from his pocket and stuck them in the pocket of Asouf's spreading robe.

"This is just an advance," he went on. "We'll pay you every month. The Archeological Department will give you a regular monthly sum. Do you know what it means, to get a salary from the government?" He waved his hand once more, and the despair in his eyes became something close to wretchedness.

Asouf gave him the ten pounds back. He wouldn't know, he said, what to do with the money. "I'll guard the wadi," he went on. "I'll guard all the wadis of Massak Satfat. I don't want money. What would I do with it here in Massak?"

The man tried to persuade him.

"But that's all wrong," he said, laughing nervously. "If you're an employee, you have to take money. It's your right. It comes from the government, a salary. You're a guard. How can I make it clear to you?"

He gave him some more cans of food, then left the wadi with his group. Asouf didn't see them again. The employee's expression, though, stuck in his mind. Was it pity? Or misery? Or helplessness? Or was it pity and misery together, because he hadn't managed to persuade him he should take a salary?

The man had been tired and clumsy. Perhaps it was his first trip over the desert and the desert had exhausted him. The Italian had had far more energy. He'd been more alert, taken a greater interest in the stones.

From that day on visitors began arriving, in the wadi forgotten for thousands of years. They came in groups, a visit every two weeks or sometimes once a month. Rarely did more than a month go by with no sign of them.

They were all foreigners, men and women, old and young, from every Christian race. They'd fall on their knees before the master jinni, take pictures in front of the temple, spend a night there sometimes, then return, leaving him some cans of foods, and cheese and dried milk, tea, sugar, and biscuits.

They were generous—more generous than the Archeological Department in the oases.

He often wondered just what lay behind the Christians' interest in the ancient paintings. He decided, finally, they must be making a pilgrimage to the Matkhandoush figures because they belonged to the same old religion; they didn't, after all, believe in the Prophet Muhammad, or kneel facing the Ka'aba as Muslims did. Veneration, and supplication and surrender, were revealed in their eyes; betrayed too by the odd way their hands moved over their faces as they examined the vast figure of the king of the wadi, and his sacred *waddan* that rose alongside him, contemplating the far horizon. The Christians stood before the masked giant exactly as Muslims stood before God. And yet his father had told him this masked jinni was his ancestor too.

ﾌﾟ

3. TWILIGHT VISITORS

He managed to drive all the herd into the big cave before the visitors arrived. The noise of the truck grew louder, and, across the expanse, he saw a cloud of dust on the horizon. The bleating of the goats rose, while the young kids leaped constantly at the mouth of the cave in protest at their early confinement. The sun vanished behind the mountain, but still poured itself on the plain opposite. At sunset it pleased the sun to clothe the desert in the red mantle of its rays.

The truck began its descent into the wadi, coming to a stop at the bottom next to the palm trees. Here and there in the dried-up bed, wild bushes had kept their greenness from the flood of the previous year. Two men got out of the truck, quite different in appearance: one tall, the other short, the tall man slim, the short man plump. They seemed about the same age. For all his weight, it was the short man who seemed the fitter and more energetic. He busied himself taking things from the truck and throwing them down on the ground, among the green bushes beneath a tall palm tree: utensils, plates, wooden boxes, canvas bags, and a large tent, which he went about pitching. The tall man approached Asouf, waving to him in greeting, and Asouf, reassured, moved toward him.

They met in the middle of the track.

"So you're the herdsman," the man said, laughing and pressing Asouf's hand warmly. "The one who's happier living in an empty desert than being with other people. They told us about you in the Wadi Aajal."

Asouf gave no answer, hastily arranging the veil over his face to hide his embarrassment. As for the man, he gazed casually out toward the mountains, his hands on his hips.

"Do you get many tourists visiting here?" he asked. "The foreigners seem to have beaten us everywhere in the desert. Wherever we've been, we've found they were there before us. These foreigners are devils."

In his belt Asouf saw a small black weapon, the sort they called a "pistol."

"Yes," he replied. "No one's come to Matkhandoush before except the Christians. This is the first time I've seen Muslims here."

The man laughed.

"Who said we were Muslims?" he remarked.

Asouf, embarrassed once more, hurriedly pulled the edges of his veil over his face. The man, seeing this, hastened to reassure him.

"I'm only joking," he said. "It's true we don't pray, or pay *zakat*, and we've never done the pilgrimage. But we're Muslims just the same."[iv]

Asouf hesitated, then asked:

"Have you come to look at the sights? I can show you places I've never shown the Christians. Places no one has ever seen."

The man started laughing helplessly.

"The sights," he said scornfully, when he'd finally recovered. "What business do we have with sights? We're sights ourselves, don't you know that? People seek us out, just the way they do you. The westerners come from beyond the seas to look at us and see how we live. Have you ever seen a sight interested in other sights?"

The blood surged to Asouf's prominent cheeks, and he didn't know what to do with his eyes and hands. The agitation reached his limbs, and he began trembling.

"The truth is," the guest said, "we're here on the track of something different—*waddan*. Can you put us on to the *waddan*? They say you even know where the birds build their nests in Massak Satfat."

Asouf looked toward the man and saw a strange glint in his eyes.

"Who told you that?" he asked, still trembling. "The *waddan* died out a long time ago, just like the gazelles. I can't take you to any *waddan*."

He was still trembling. The man seemed displeased by his answer, but he held himself in.

"Well, then," he said, gazing suspiciously at Asouf, "since you evidently don't know where the *waddan* lives, you can show us the other sights."

They moved toward the tent.

"But I can't sleep without meat," the man went on. "How can I eat my supper without meat?"

His fat friend, who still hadn't shaken hands with Asouf, laughed.

"He's not joking," the man said. "He hasn't slept even one night without meat, not since his mother bore him. They say he came into the world with a piece of meat in his mouth. Lamb's meat." He laughed. "I've known him all my life," he went on, "and I'm telling you, he's likely to eat himself if he doesn't find some meat to eat at night." He laughed again.

"You'd better not sleep close to him. He might crawl out and eat you. Ha, ha!"

"God help us," Asouf murmured simply. "Is he so fond of meat?"

The tall man answered, gnashing his teeth together, his eyes shining once more with their strange glint.

"Is there anything in the world tastier than meat? Everything begins and ends with meat. Woman's meat too. Have you ever tasted a woman's meat?"

Asouf shook his head, the anxiety shining in his eyes.

"You're a poor devil, then," the man went on, laughing. "You've never enjoyed a woman's meat. It's the tastiest of all. Apart, that is, from gazelle's meat and lamb's meat—and the meat from the *waddan*." He laughed again. "Every sort of meat's tasty. Have you ever eaten—"

"No," Asouf cried out, dismayed. "No! I haven't had any sort of meat. I don't eat meat."

"You don't eat meat? What sort of life's that?"

The man reflected for a while.

"Well," he said finally, "it makes sense. If you don't eat meat, then you have to live apart from other people. I see now why you've chosen to live in this empty wilderness. If a man doesn't eat meat, then he doesn't live. You're not alive at all. You're dead!"

Asouf retreated a couple of steps, as if about to flee.

"I heard," he said, "that you've eaten up all the lambs in the north. Is that true?"

"Ha, ha! Listen to him! Yes, it's true enough!"

"And they say you've wiped out all the gazelle herds in the Red Hamada. Is that true as well?"

"Ha, ha! Listen to him! Yes, it's true. I'm proud to say I personally ate the last gazelle in the northern desert. Do you have a problem with that? Where's the harm?"

Asouf was silent for a few moments.

"There aren't any *waddan* in these deserts," he answered, in a perplexed tone. "The *waddan* died out long ago. I have some goats. I can slaughter a goat for you."

The man threw himself back and laughed. The weapon rose prominently on his waist. Then he spat several times on the ground.

"Ha!" he sneered. "You call that proper meat? It's filthy stuff. Even the dogs won't touch it unless they have to. The wolves are ashamed to eat it! I don't eat goat's meat. I've never eaten goat's meat. However bad things have gotten, I've never had to sink that low!"

And with that he bent hastily over a dried-up bush and started retching.

The fat man reproached Asouf.

"You see what you've done to your guest? He can't stand goat's meat."

"But what can I do?" Asouf said. "Goats are all I have."

"Don't mention goats again. People like that, with a sickly hunger for meat, mostly don't eat goat's meat. There are plenty like him in the north."

The man began opening the boxes and taking out the contents.

"The best thing," he went on, a sly smile appearing in his eyes, "would be for you to show us the caves where the *waddan* are. Not slaughter stringy goats. Where do the *waddan* hide out here in these mountains? You wouldn't miss their lairs, would you? You even know those races of ancient men on the rocks, and you talk with the jinn on moonlit nights. Or so they told us. That lone bedouin, they said, is close friends with the jinn."

He laughed, without raising his head from the utensils and plates and other baggage. Then he winked at his friend, and the two began walking southward across the winding wadi in search of firewood. Asouf watched as they talked together in low voices, bent over the dry sticks.

He returned to his herd, thrusting the kids back into the cave. He saw the two men look indifferently at the paintings on the tall rock. Then he heard them shrieking with laughter. The meat eater was making loud, sarcastic comments, and being answered by similar laughter from his fat friend. The echo rang throughout the high western mountains.

They returned with a bundle of sticks. The fat man flung them down next to the tent, then shouted to Asouf.

"Hey, you, whatever your name is. We're going to take a look at the wadis, before the sun goes down. Keep an eye on our things and our food."

They leaped into the truck and headed off toward the wadi leading to Abrahoh. The sun slipped behind the mountains crowned with their pillars of rocks, and shadows spread through the plain opposite, like troops of the jinn.

He still seemed to hear those shrieks of laughter, and those whispers, echoing among the rocks of the wadi— sounds that disturbed him for reasons he couldn't fathom. He felt his heart beating.

4. A Devil Called Man

The heart is the guide for those who don't understand people. The heart is the fire by which the bedouin's guided in the desert of this world, just as a man lost in the wilderness will be guided by the Idi star. All other stars transform and move, shift and vanish. Only this one stays firm until morning. Idi's like the heart. It doesn't deceive.

His father, when he was alive, urged him always to listen to his heart. He'd have Asouf sit there in front of him on the moonlit summer nights, and teach him the *Fatiha* to help him with his prayers. Each day he had to memorize one of the verses. Then, when he'd memorized the whole chapter, his father said: "Listen to your heart. What would a desert man do if he lost his heart? If we lose that, we wander lost in the world, because a desert man doesn't understand the wiles of men."

He'd also, before meeting that dreadful death, taught him the *Ikhlas* chapter. They'd lived alone in the desert, alone in all their movements and wanderings. Asouf couldn't remember any human neighbor from the day he was born. He did recall how once, during his childhood, a family had suddenly borne down on them. It had come from Tadrart to settle in the high wadis, in a year when the sky lavished rains

on Massak. He woke next morning to noise and bustle, to find
his father packing, saddling the camels and preparing them
to travel. What had woken him, though, wasn't the movement
or the clattering of utensils and dishes. It was the quarrel
between his parents, provoked, he gathered, by the sudden
trip. His mother had an acute sense of shame and set great
store by what people thought of other people. For her the
sudden departure was an affront to the new guests in the wadi
and brought shame on themselves. "I'd rather have jinn as
neighbors than people," he heard his father retort. "God
protect us from the evil of people!" Often, too, his father
would recite a *muwwal* he'd heard sung, he said, by the Sufis
in the community at Uwaynat:

> The desert is a true treasure
> for him who seeks refuge
> from men and the evil of men.
> In it is contentment,
> in it is death and all you seek.

As he recited, he'd lower his eyelids and rock from side to side,
in imitation of the Sufi *shaykhs* in their fervor and ecstasy.

He'd go hunting with his father, and on his trips to the
pastures. His father taught him how to break the wild camels,
until they grew obedient and quick. In Massak Satfat he
showed him how to hunt the *waddan*, taught him how to aim
his gun. He'd wake Asouf early so as to strike at the herds of
gazelle feeding freely on the plains in the darkness of dawn.

At night he liked to make green tea and talk to Asouf
about the qualities of the different animals and birds in the
desert. He'd remove any stones, lie down on the sand, then
unveil his mouth and his beard shot through with white. He'd
smile, then say:

"What do you think? What does the gazelle tell himself when he sees the enemy of all creatures? He says, 'the plain.' And what does the *waddan* say to himself when he sees the enemy of all creatures? He says, 'the mountain.' The mountain's a trap for the gazelle, the plain's a trap for the *waddan*."

He'd raise his head toward the skies and sing a sad *muwwal*, then return to his old story about the *waddan*.

"I saw a *waddan* who'd lost his way on the wide plains. I chased him, on my camel, until he was exhausted. And do you know what he did, as his strength drained away? He turned and attacked the camel, thrusting at it with those vicious horns of his, until the camel took fright and turned back. I had to dismount and take on the furious beast. All I had was the rope in my hand. I tried to choke him with it, but he thrust at me and flung me to the ground. I grasped his long horns. And, believe me, I've never known anything stronger than a *waddan*'s horns. God, how strong they are! With one movement he plucked me up and flung me through the air. Then he came at me with his devilish weapon, and I only just swerved in time from the sharp tips. He pawed savagely at the stones, and in that short moment I saw rancor and wretchedness together in his eyes. I saw stubbornness and wildness, and many other things I didn't even understand. His lips were covered with foam, his shaggy coat was caked with dung and mud. Knowing I'd never get the better of him with my bare hands, I leaped up and ran to my camel to snatch the rifle hanging from the saddle."

He fell silent suddenly, gazing into the thick darkness of the wilderness. There was a sudden wretchedness in his eyes. He got up and clasped his hands over his chest, still looking into the darkness and space.

"I forgot to tell you," he said, "that our battle happened

in a wadi well away from the mountains. The *waddan* knew he couldn't escape because he was so far from his mountain stronghold. In the middle of the wadi there was a small hill covered with high, smooth rocks. When he saw I'd taken my rifle, he climbed the rocks in a single swift movement, then leaped to the ground and broke his neck. The blood gushed out from his nostrils, and, after he was dead, his eyes were open and that strange look was still there—the mixture of wretchedness and rancor and helplessness."

"Did you slaughter it," Asouf asked, "and make its flesh lawful?"

"How could I slaughter an animal that had killed itself? In any case, he'd died at once. I told you, his neck was broken. He was already dead."[vi]

He sighed, put on some sticks to feed the dwindling fire, then said sadly:

"I can't get that strange, possessed *waddan* out of my mind. How could I forget that fearful, despairing look he gave me when he saw the rifle in my hands and knew all hope of escape was gone? Poor, possessed *waddan*!"

He waited until the moon had risen, then told Asouf how the *waddan* was the spirit of the mountains. Once long ago, he said, the mountain desert waged constant war with the sandy desert, and the heavenly gods would descend to earth to separate the pair, calming the fire of enmity between them. But no sooner had the gods left the battlefield, and the rains stopped pouring down, than war would break out once more between the two eternal enemies. One day, the gods grew angry in their high heavens and sent down their punishment on the fighters. They froze the mountains in Massak Satfat, and they stopped the persistent advance of the sands on the borders of Massak Mallat. Then the sands found a way to enter the spirit of the gazelles, while the mountains found a way into the spirit of the *waddan*. And from that day on, the *waddan* was possessed by the spirit of the mountains.

Asouf reflected on this tale.

"But," he said, "gazelles and *waddan* don't fight now."

His father let out a great laugh. Then, gazing at the magical moon as it rose from out of the heart of darkness, he said in a mysterious tone: "That's because God visited a greater disaster on earth, one that fought the two sides at once. Man came, to be the enemy of gazelles and *waddan* alike. The gods had grown tired of all the silly complaints. Sometimes the sands would rise to make their case to the heavens—it was the mountains, they said, that had started things. And sometimes it was the mountain tops that would go to the gods, complaining of the raids made by the sands. So the gods, in their anger, punished them both with a devil called man. They placed the matter in his hands, and he came to live in the wadi between the two. Now the gods could have a little peace at last, and they've heard no more complaints since."

He turned to Asouf and went on in the same mysterious tone.

"How can I be a neighbor of men? Your mother keeps scolding me—she wants me to go back and live near the tribe in Abrahoh. She says she's lonely and she weeps at night. You know how she weeps. I'm the one, she says, who's the jinni, the devil, and not the other people. But I can't live near anyone. That's what my grandfather taught me, and that's what I must teach you. All I want is peace. Do you understand?"

Then he raised his voice in the same sad *muwwal*.

~~

5. THE PRICE OF SOLITUDE

For the people of the Tassili the hunting of the waddan *is
unlucky. The hunter accordingly murmurs spells, places a
stone on his head and leaps around on all fours before
embarking on the hunt.*
—Henri Lhote, A la découverte des fresques du Tassili

But he didn't long enjoy the contentment of solitude, there
in the desert with his father. The old man went off to hunt
the *waddan* in the mountains of western Massis, and was
destined not to return. After they'd waited some days for him,
his mother gave voice to her fears.

"Your father wouldn't stay away without some reason. It's
over a week since he left."

Asouf took dates and water and set out after him. His
father was unarmed now, which was why, instead of hunting
the gazelles in Massak Mallat, he'd had to go in pursuit of the
charmed *waddan* on the tops of the harsh, rugged mountains.
Since that incident he'd described to Asouf, he'd become
wary of hunting the *waddan*, and would never venture to the
majestic heights until he'd recited all the Quranic verses he'd
memorized, repeated, in Hausa, all the spells of the African

magicians, then hung around his neck all the snakeskin amulets he'd bought from soothsayers traveling in caravans from Kano. The day before he left, he'd sit murmuring his spells and keep strict silence otherwise, refusing to answer their questions. He'd sleep outside the tent too, to avoid having to speak with either of them, then leave at dawn on his camel, empty-handed. Yes, unarmed and empty-handed, for he'd run out of ammunition for his old rifle, and the merchant caravans traveled to Sudan or to Agades only rarely now. Months would go by without a caravan from the land of the black people passing through. He'd lost his connections, too, with the people from the oases of the Wadi Aajal, or Ghat, or Uwaynat, or Marzouq—especially since news had spread that the Italians had invaded their shores, with plans to penetrate south into the desert. This had raised the price of ammunition and made the use of weapons a forbidden, hazardous business. Every bedouin in the desert would rather hide a bullet in the pupil of his eye, ready to use it to defend his children at the dreadful moment the enemy launched its invasion of the desert—for, if the Italians did come, they'd enter every tent. Isolated though the bedouins were, in their southern wilderness, news of the invaders still came to them on the winds, as rumors always do among desert tribes—rumors of marriage and divorce and scandal, of death and the birth of new children. Nothing's ever secret in the desert, no matter what lonely spot you choose.

Once, though, when his father was away, Asouf's mother had whispered to him of some bullets his father had hidden in the hunters' cave. He was, she said, careful how he used them. He'd laughed that day, remembering what his father had once said: "A man in the desert must be sparing with two things: water and bullets." In the desert, he'd gone on, water and bullets were like air, the very foundation of life. If you ran out of the first, you'd die of thirst, and if you ran out of the second, some enemy, man or beast or snake, would strike you down. Water and bullets were the life blood of a lone man. He could go without anything else, but not those. Asouf had no doubt his mother was right. His father had hidden those bullets in the cave against a day of misfortune, so he'd be able to affirm his strength and manhood. He'd shoot a bullet in the enemy's face before he died himself—he wouldn't let them gloat as they dragged him along, trussed up like a lamb! It's no shame to die with your hands around a rifle. The shame is when you die bound like a lamb. The shame is to fall alive into the enemy's hands, to be a prisoner. No one falls prisoner except the coward or the man without a weapon.

That was why his father had chosen to hide a few bullets in the hunters' cave and go off to hunt the *waddan* unarmed. And that was why he'd died in such a fearful way. If he hadn't been so resolved not to be taken alive, hoarding his bullets against the day of misfortune, he would have been spared that hideous death.

For some days Asouf followed his father's tracks, and, when he found the traces of that struggle with the *waddan* in the Wadi Aynesis, fear gripped him. He followed the signs of the encounter, along the wadi, until he found blood spots on some stones, then drops of blood, widely scattered, on the sand in the wadi's heart. Was the wounded creature the *waddan* or his father? He had no way of knowing. The traces would appear, then disappear, would veer left toward the rugged slope with its covering of sharp black stones, then back to the sandy bed where palm trees and wild grasses grew here and there. Under a high palm tree the battle had grown fiercer. Traces were thick and numerous, one on the other. Had the old man tried to tie the savage beast to the trunk of this tall palm, before the *waddan* at last prevailed and dragged him a few steps across the wadi? Or—oh God!—had he gripped the beast by the horns, done what he himself had so often warned his son never to do? Nothing, his father had said, drove the *waddan* to frenzy like gripping him by the horns. It didn't matter how strong you were, how stirred by the hope of victory. If you once tried that, then the battle was lost. The *waddan*'s madness lay in his horns. All his hidden savagery would wake, would boil over, and he'd launch his ferocious attack. The *waddan* was trying to escape now—he'd veered off toward the mountain. The wadi was getting deeper, the mountains higher. The *waddan* was drawing him on, toward that ugly, mysterious summit!

Asouf's heart started to pound as he sent his gaze upward. There, he sensed, something had happened—beneath the peak, or on the very top, or somewhere on the slopes. There were no traces of struggle visible now. He ran, panting, across the narrow wadi, between the two mountains. Ominous shadows lay over the pass. He turned left, scrambled swiftly up the steep slope. Suddenly a fetid smell seemed to assail his nostrils. His heart leaped. Nausea swept through him, and pain beat inside his head. The nearer his mad ascent took him toward the summit, the higher and sharper and blacker the rocks became. He was clambering on all fours now. The fetid smell grew stronger. Then, just beneath the ill-omened summit, near a long rock stretching several spans across the slope, he found the old man, lying on his back, his face toward the sky and his eyes empty. The face was blue, and large blue flies hovered over him. There was no sign of bleeding, not a single spot of blood, except for some scratches on the arms stretched out alongside his body.

The possessed *waddan* had caused him to break his neck, just as he himself had once made that other *waddan* do the same.

~~

6. THE GIRL

In Southern Libya, on the heights of the Nasamouniyyin, the Gramants live in a place rich with beasts. They are a people who shun others, fearing to speak with them. They use no weapons at all, and have no knowledge of how to defend themselves.
—Herodotus, *Histories*

He too had a bitter experience with the *waddan*. After his father's death, he took charge of affairs, herding the goats, looking over the camels in the nearby wadis, bringing in wood, going off to meet the caravans to barter goats for sacks of barley and dates. Haggling didn't come easily to a young man who lacked the proper means to address people. He had no knowledge of people's natures, of their character or behavior. How could he have, when he'd passed his whole life remote and apart from them, when he was afraid of them? His sense of helplessness reduced him to panic. How was he to talk with them, mix with them, when the mere thought of going near them terrified him?

The first time he stood a good way off, watching the long caravan as it wound its way along the path through the wadis, as it climbed the rugged mountains, before veering sometimes right and sometimes left; until, finally, the line of patient camels, laden with burdens and goods, melted into the unknown horizon and vanished. The caravan was gone, and he'd been unable to approach it.

He returned home defeated, to his mother's bitter scolding. Weeping, she said he was like a girl. Then she said: "It's not your fault. Your father, God rest his soul, turned you into a camel frightened by men's shadows." He didn't sleep at all that night.

It would be weeks, months maybe, before another caravan passed through, and the store of grain was dwindling. There was only enough left for ten days. After a few days he packed his clothes and drove his herds to the road that linked Marzouq with Kano, three days' journey away. There he decided to await the merchant caravans. He camped in the wadi, letting the herds pasture among the wild bushes, and, several times a day, climbed the hill to look out over the road. On the fourth day he saw the caravan on the far horizon, a mirage dancing around it. He tied a small bag of wheat to the neck of a fat, sturdy she-goat, a bag of barley to the neck of the fierce, graceful he-goat who'd broken the ribs of the kids by butting and attacking them, then climbed the hill, tethering the beasts to stakes he'd sunk in an open space where the caravan would pass. Then he went back to his spot on the slope, took up a position behind the rocks, and waited.

The she-goat tried to free herself, and, when she finally gave up the attempt, shattered the silence with bleating and complaint. As for the unruly he-goat, he seemed more patient, gazing into the bare open spaces with sad and anxious looks. Then, lifting his head toward the horizon and the caravan, he awaited his fate.

The caravan drew up, and the men gathered around the two goats, gazing over the empty spaces for the owner. At that he emerged from his hiding place and walked alongside the rocks overlooking the wadi. They waved to him in greeting, and he, in response, raised his hand to the level of his face, then brought it down in a quick movement. He was highly nervous. Sweat was trickling down his neck and back, and he didn't know what to do with his hands. He tried to hide his embarrassment by fixing his turban on his head. They beckoned to him to approach, but he pretended not to notice.

One of the men left the group and started walking toward him. Quivering with terror now, he jumped up and vanished behind the rocks, leaping among the stones like a *waddan*. Then he stood panting on the slope, covered in sweat and shame. His mother had been right—he was a girl. A man doesn't flee to avoid meeting other men. Shyness was for girls, that was what his mother said. He'd never seen girls, never seen the shyness in their eyes. Shame on him! Now, for the first time, he felt resentment toward his father. His father it was who'd implanted this fear of people in him, fear deep enough to drive every girl in the world to flee from men, for ever more!

He went back and hid behind a rock. He saw the men laughing and arguing. Then the caravan moved on. The winding road veered west, then finally disappeared among the mountain tops.

They took the two goats with them, leaving him two medium-size sacks, one of wheat, the other of barley.

7. A Phantom from the Himalayas

The two visitors didn't return until the next morning. They brought their truck to a halt alongside the tent, then got out, the tall one first. He was disheveled, his face pale, and he looked as wilted as if back from some long trip—as though he'd crossed the desert from Timbuktu to the Naffousa Mountain! He approached Asouf and held out a strong, rough hand.

"We haven't introduced ourselves," he said. "My name's Cain Adam, and my friend here's called Masoud, Masoud al-Dabbashi."

He let his gaze wander out across the wadi, then lifted his head toward the sky and launched a volley of complaint.

"The sun's been beating down ever since this morning. I'm telling you, it's hell! God, what can you do to get away from this desert sun?"

He managed a desperate, mournful smile, then abruptly changed the subject.

"We've put up with the sun," he said. "But we can't go on without the *waddan*." He scowled, then continued, angrily now. "All right, a joke's a joke. For two days now you've made us go without *waddan* meat. I've never, in all my life, had to go two days without meat."

31

Asouf wanted to protest, to counter the accusation, to explain. But he didn't know how. He reflected for some time, then said:

"There aren't any *waddan* here. And besides, it's difficult to hunt. Very difficult."

"Leave that to me," Cain burst out. "Difficult or not. Just show me where they are. Then we'll see."

"The *waddan* only lives up on the tops of the hardest mountains."

"So you admit it's there! In the mountains!"

Asouf was confused.

"It might be there in the mountains," he stammered, after a struggle with himself. "I don't know." He wiped away the sweat with the sleeve of his gown.

"Who lives in these mountains besides you?" Cain asked. "They told us in the oases there was just one human being living in Massak Mallat, along with whole tribes of jinn and herds of *waddan*." He turned to his companion. "Did you hear that?" he yelled. "The fellow's admitted there are *waddan* in the mountains!"

Asouf didn't know where to put himself. He cursed the day he was born, and the day this girlish shyness had taken possession of him. How was he to take back what he'd just admitted? He couldn't find the right words to protest. How was he, who'd never mixed with people, to make his case to others?

Masoud al-Dabbashi produced a scrap of dry meat. He offered Cain a piece and started munching the rest.

"Eat some of this," he said, "before you finally go crazy and start raving. I don't want to have to nurse you out here in the desert."

He turned and addressed Asouf.

"The jinn take hold of his mind, do you know that, if he doesn't get meat?"

"Yes, I know," Asouf replied. "My father told me about it. A craving for meat brings madness. People can't help themselves."

The two guests exchanged a meaningful look, then burst into hearty laughter. Cain tore off a piece of his dried meat and offered it to Asouf.

"They told us you mix with jinni women in the caves," he said. "But they didn't tell us you were a sage."

Asouf moved back a step, as if fleeing from the meat. He laid his hand on his chest in a gesture of thanks, then murmured, with repugnance: "No. No, I don't eat meat."

The two men exchanged further looks.

"Do you really mean that?" Cain asked censoriously. "Is there anyone in the world who doesn't eat meat? Apart, that is, from those phantoms they say live on the tops of the Himalayas?"

He came closer and tried to thrust the piece of meat into Asouf's mouth.

"Eat it, go on! This isn't meat from your filthy goats. This is dried lamb. It tastes—like gazelle meat, like *waddan*."

Asouf refused, retreating once more, but Cain wouldn't stop prodding him. Masoud intervened.

"Don't force it on the man," he told Cain. "Perhaps he really means it. Maybe there are Himalayan phantoms in our desert too!"

8. THE VOW

To feed his mother and himself, while living free in God's wide desert, he had to do more than conquer himself, more than find a way of addressing the human devils and offer them his goats, so as to gain his food of wheat and barley from those dreadful hands like the claws of beasts. He had to venture on something further, something written on the brow of those fated to be born and live in the desert—the hunting of the *waddan*.

His father, God rest his soul, had liked to talk of this as they sat together on summer nights, out in the open air.

"If you've chosen to live alone," he told him, "you have to hunt the *waddan* alone. It's a thing like thirst, like hunger, like life in the wilderness; it's the fate of isolation, the fate of the desert. God has set a price on everything."

His father changed, even so, from the time that stubborn *waddan* killed itself. He became dejected, depressed, preoccupied. He'd sing those sad, passionate *muwwals*, paying no attention when Asouf spoke to him or asked him a question. Often, when Asouf went with him to the Tadrart mountains or the desert of Massak Mallat, they wouldn't exchange a single word. He'd sit behind the camel's saddle, listen to the long, mournful *muwwals* that seemed to have no end. Something was burning his father's heart, and he was striving to put out the fire with these *muwwals* that only burned the son's heart too, so that he wept there in his place behind the saddle. Why did these songs tug so at his heart? Why did they bring him such unbearable pain? Was it because they expressed man's helplessness in the desert? Or because they made him sense the desert's cruelty? Or because they told how the destiny of a lone man was only sorrow and hardship? Was it because they rent the veil of illusion, made plain that, if a man lost his links with people, he'd lose his links with himself; that if he lost others he'd lose his own self, which would come to lack all point? Was it because of some message those *muwwals* bore: that salvation and freedom meant the desert, and the desert merely meant death? Was he weeping because his sad father's *muwwals* somehow captured the nature of their strange life in the eternal desert, where nothing else seemed to exist in the world?

Or were these simply his own imaginings? Did his father's sorrow just spring from pain, because life's cruelty forced him to hunt the *waddan* against his will? The scorching south wind sucked the tears that trickled slowly down his cheeks, and the sands, thirsty for moisture, swallowed the blood that dripped from his lips—the lips his teeth tore without his even noticing, because nothing could extinguish or suck away the fire ablaze within him.

His father started teaching him to hunt while he was still very young, as soon as he was ten. That wasn't, after all, too early for desert boys. He didn't, though, teach him to hunt the *waddan*. He had him fire a rifle at rocks and stones in the mountains, then he set him on the saddle on the camel's back and spent several days with him in the plains of Massak Mallat, where herds of gazelle roamed to graze. He'd wake him in the darkness of dawn, sprinkle drops of cold water on his face to bring him fully awake—or, as he liked to say, to get his eyes open—then, tugging him by the hand, he'd go down with him to the wide wadis, where gazelles abounded in the darkness. Although there were plenty of gazelles in the desert then, his father had made it a strict rule never to hunt more than one gazelle each trip. That way, he maintained, the soul of the gazelle would become stronger and firmer. It would find itself protected by the shield of the Quran, and by the talismans of magicians and amulets of soothsayers, and by the incantations of devout sages. A famous magician in Kano had warned him against hunting the gazelle too hard. And he'd told him, too, of the bands of soothsayers who duped the unwary, claiming their amulets would permit the wholesale slaughter of wild beasts. Such men, the magician said, were mere charlatans, practicing false wiles no person of sense would swallow. His father would praise this man, saying he'd never known a magician more truthful. It was for that, he went on, that the man was so famous through the length and breadth of the desert, so that people sought him out from Ghadames to Timbuktu, from the Naffousa Mountain to Agades.

When he'd learned to shoot a gazelle in the darkness of dawn, his father gave him a wondrous present: the Tamba sandals embellished by the nimble fingers of the girls of Tamanrasset, who poured into the designs their passion and their longing to meet the knight of their dreams. Their feelings overflowed from the lines and decorations and drawings. The girl who'd made those sandals must have been deeply in love—so he was assured by his mother, who was well able to read the embroidery of young girls on leather. "The throbbings of a girl's heart," she told him, "are in her palm, and her passions on the tips of her fingers. Every old woman knows how to read this alphabet, whether it's written on animal skins, or on canvas, or woven with woolen threads. The hidden letters of this language are only revealed to wise old women."

So much for the gazelles. With the *waddan* things were different—here he ventured only much later, when he was already fifteen. The delay had to do with his father's secret links with the *waddan*, links ancient and inscrutable, present long before the matter of the beast that killed itself. Whenever he asked to go with his father to hunt the *waddan*, his father would draw back, finding, always, some reason to put off the time. And when Asouf persisted, saying he wanted to learn, his father still kept fobbing him off, finding some special reason to refuse. One bitter winter night, Asouf recalled, the three of them were gathered around the fire in the herdsmen's cave, and he took the chance to repeat his request once more. The old man gazed long into his eyes, then exchanged a still longer look with his mother. Then he bowed his head, hiding his face in the blazing fire. But Asouf had read in his father's eyes an unease he hadn't seen before, and in his mother's eyes too; and he sensed for the first time there was some secret involved. He wanted to ask his mother about it, but she forestalled him.

"Why do you keep asking your father to take you to kill *waddan*?" she said one day. "Can't you see it hurts him?"

"But why does it hurt him?" Asouf asked anxiously. "I just don't understand!"

But she didn't reveal the secret—not until he'd been

with his father on several failed hunts for the *waddan* in the nearby mountains. On the first trip, they'd followed the tracks of a whole herd, catching up with it, finally, in the bottom of a wadi. Then the chase began, but it produced nothing. The herd simply vanished, hiding itself behind rocks on the mountain tops. His father, he realized, had fired to miss, deliberately frightening the herd. The second time they caught up with a fat female, who stood there in front of them. His father stopped, exchanged a furtive look with the beast, then turned to Asouf and said she was pregnant—and to hunt a pregnant animal from the herd was a great sin. So they returned empty-handed. The third time he himself managed to spot three *waddan* grazing among bushes that grew on the slope. His father had to give him the rifle, but, as the boy took aim, he coughed loudly, and the *waddan*, taking fright, scurried off, taking refuge among the rocks of the nearby mountain.

He exchanged a look with his father. Then, as he handed back the rifle, he said: "Why don't you want me to learn how to hunt the *waddan*? And if you're so anxious I shouldn't, why do you tire yourself out, and tire me out, with these ridiculous trips? Why don't you tell me the truth?"

His father made no answer to all this. He simply bowed his head and pulled his turban tight around his face until it shielded his eyes, then returned home with him without saying a single word.

After this his mother felt bound to confess the truth. His father had gone out early one day to look over the camels in the sandy plains of the desert, and she called out to him to stay behind. She flung some sticks on the fire, drew her oil-spattered cloak tight around herself and began churning the milk in a skin. Then she briefly revealed the secret.

"Your father," she told him, "doesn't want you to spill the *waddan*'s blood because of a vow he made long ago, before you were born. He was hunting on the slopes of Aynesis, and his foot slipped. He found himself hanging between earth and sky, holding on to a rock with his legs dangling down into a chasm. He'd given up all hope. But the very beast he'd been fighting and trying to kill brought him out and saved him from death. Now do you understand? He vowed he'd never again go near the *waddan*, and that he wouldn't teach his children to hunt it. But he became hungry. We were hungry together in those harsh drought years before you were born. I was pregnant then, and he had to break his vow and hunt. He wept before he did it. I heard him with my own ears, weeping at night. He left in the morning, and he came back with a large *waddan*. We skinned it and ate it, filling our stomachs at last. He said he'd broken his vow and the spirit of the mountains would punish him for it. But he wouldn't, he assured me, teach his son, if he were granted a son, how to hunt the *waddan*. Do you understand now, you stubborn boy? I told you not to keep pestering him. It hurts him."

9. THE PIT

*O Lord, thou hast brought up my soul from the grave: thou
hast kept me alive, that I should not go down to the pit.*
—Psalms, 30:3

*Fulfillment springs from patience.
Patience springs from power.
Power springs from authority.*
—Al-Niffari, *"Fulfillment"*

When the possessed beast broke his father's neck, Asouf
remembered his mother's words about the vow. Then
he promptly forgot it. Youth is the devil's companion; it
tempted him and he thought no more of the matter. One day
the devil smuggled three *waddan* into his herd of goats, then
sat watching him from the mountain top.

It happened a few years after his father's death. Asouf was
grazing his herd in the south the Wadi Matkhandoush,
where the waters from rivers and floods had formed deep
gullies, before the wadi veered to the right, then disappeared
among the high western mountains, among sheer rocks that
stood like phantoms guarding the stony desert and keeping

watch over the palm trees in the depths. He lay down under a rock on the slopes, watching the stubborn goats as they tried to reach up to the green branches of the palms. Laughing, he saw how a greedy she-goat strove to reach the green tips of a tree that was simply too tall for her. Alongside this tree stood an upright stone with a narrow top. The goat scaled this in two leaps, and a moment later, from its comfortable seat, was stretching its neck to the very top of the wretched tree to destroy its green cap. Meanwhile, at the other end of the wadi, near the faded wild thickets, a fine-looking he-goat, crowned with a pair of great curved horns, was busily flirting with a comely, silver-colored she-goat, while alongside another he-goat, ugly and disheveled, looked resentfully on. The she-goat was responding to the play of the fine male, twisting her neck, brushing his nose with her own in brief kisses, then plunging her head into the dried-up bushes, with a busy pretense of eating the plants. These apparent rejections excited the fine, handsome he-goat, who ventured to approach closer. He'd advance a step and plunge his head down next to hers, pretending to eat too, then thrust his nose forward to snatch a kiss from her. Then back he'd go to view her, hesitant and tentative, from behind. He'd gaze around the pasture, exchange a threatening look with the other he-goat, then once more nuzzle the skittish female, until he'd reached her back part and could snuffle her smell.

Still the other he-goat looked restlessly on. There was fear in the gaze, along with wariness and surprise. Suddenly it dawned on Asouf that the fine, splendid goat lover wasn't a goat at all. It was a *waddan*! He read the signs in the eyes of the other he-goat, the true aspirant.

A huge *waddan*, gray in color, with silver hairs shining through his thick coat. A long beard dangling from his chin, his head crowned with a pair of great curved horns. How had he failed to see that this "goat," which had roused his admiration, whose moves and flirtations with the she-goat he'd been following so closely, wasn't a goat at all, but the mighty *waddan*?

In the heart of the wadi, in among the herd, he saw two more *waddan* roaming with the goats. His father had never told him, and nor had his mother, that the *waddan* might feel comfortable among ordinary goats, choosing to graze serenely alongside them. And that the males of this shy, secretive animal might venture on flirtation with the she-goats!

A few weeks before his father's death, the two of them had gone together to Abrahoh to bring back wood on a team of camels. "Don't think animals can't understand," his father had said, "just because they can't speak the way you do. They're cleverer than either of us!" That was his response to Asouf's teasing when he saw the great tenderness his father was lavishing on his piebald camel. He'd talk to the beast during day and night alike, at dawn before he prayed the dawn prayer, at noon before he started eating his lunch, at night before he went to sleep. He'd fondle the hairs on the camel's body, stroke his long neck, and, with the most tender care, wipe the foam from the big, dangling lips. Then he'd hug the beast's head and say: "Did you ever, in the whole desert, see a more beautiful camel? One that was more obedient, braver and more patient? Did you ever see one that was more intelligent and sensible? God, how beautiful he is! Look at this piebald camel—his eyes, his teeth, his slender neck, his legs. Everything's in proportion, everything's graceful. Even his belly isn't like other camels' bellies. It's slim and small and smooth. In fact he doesn't really have a belly, because he's a noble camel. A noble camel doesn't have a belly, he won't desert his beloved for the sake of his belly, like those other greedy beasts. This piebald's the beloved of all the she-camels in the Sahara. Yesterday I had a token of admiration and praise, passed on by a roving herdsman, from the comely she-camels of Tamanghast. They'd sent him a new halter, decorated with different colors and embroidered with gold threads. All the she-camels know his worth, and love him, because he's the noblest, most beautiful camel in all the Sahara." With that he'd go and fetch the beast a handful of the barley he took care to bring along especially on all his trips, and he'd feed him from his outstretched hands. He'd spoil his camel quite outrageously, even letting him drink from his own scarce supply of water. In the desert the store of water is the store of life. No rider dares be liberal with it, endlessly threatened as he is with thirst. Amid all this playful pampering, Asouf's father would turn to him regularly with the same piece of advice: "Always take the greatest care of your camel. If you don't love him, he won't love you. If you don't understand him, he won't understand you—and then he won't save you when the going gets rough. Animals are more faithful than people."

He'd told him, that night, how a faithful camel once managed to save his owner from enemies who'd attacked him on one of their raids. They'd made a circle all around him, and he'd almost fallen into their hands. It was the gallantry and courage of his camel that saved him. The camel broke through the enemies' siege heedless of the stabs of spears and knives, then went on, the blood flowing, until he'd brought his owner to safety. Then he knelt down, stretched out his neck and died.

His father concluded his tales of animals that night with the melancholy *muwwal* on gazelles, which he never tired of repeating whenever the moon rose a few paces higher than the ground, covering the wilderness with its pale silver beams and turning it to a place of magic and mystery. He'd love then to weep over the gazelles, murmuring, as if to himself: "How beautiful their shape is, their bodies so graceful, so smooth. Magic overflows from their eyes. They're the loveliest creatures in the world. They're the spirit of the sandy desert, its vast stretches, with its calm and composure and the magic of its moon. We see the impossible in the gazelle, we see freedom, and that's why no creature can ever hope to catch it alive. The thought torments me, that I've never in my life held a live gazelle in my hands." Tears would glisten in his eyes, which he'd cover with his veil. Then he'd go on, through his tears: "I just don't understand. Why should this wicked creature man chase such an angel, to kill it and fill his belly with it? Would man die of hunger if he never killed a gazelle? And why should man be so hungry that he feels he has to spill the blood of this lovely creature? Maybe that's why God punishes us, refuses to let us catch it alive." As for the *waddan*, if ever it should be mentioned, he'd say in a mysterious tone: "The *waddan*'s different. I fear the *waddan*."

The *waddan* was intelligent. It had grown less elusive over the past few years, since peace settled on the wadis of Massak Satfat and they'd had less to fear from hunters and shepherds' dogs and the rifles of adventurers. No one had killed a *waddan* in these parts since the time of his father's death, and the animal, feeling secure, had come down from its fortresses in the high mountains, venturing to share the sparse food with the herds of goats in the lower pastures.

The vow stopped the son from following his father in hunting the *waddan*; his father, after all, had died because he'd broken the sacred pledge. Vows are no light matter, and the *waddan* knows that. How could he not know it, when he's the spirit of the mountains? Spirits are from the spirit of God, and they see everything. They know what man keeps hidden deep in his heart, and that's why they're so utterly, amazingly sure of themselves. The splendid *waddan* was butting now with the disheveled ugly creature, the jealous he-goat. The he-goat was pawing the ground with his front hooves, making his challenge, ready for battle. God! Who ever saw a *waddan* butting with a he-goat?

He found himself taking his stick and rope, and slipping into the heart of the wadi. There he crept among the rocks and wild bushes until he overlooked the spot where the *waddan* was pursuing the comely she-goat, not deigning to notice the challenge of the jealous, resentful he-goat. It moved proudly and majestically, and the silvery ore, strewn over its gray hairs, glittered in the sunlight, adding to its air of awesome mystery.

He didn't know what made him start moving, on all fours, toward the possessed animal. He didn't even know what he was trying to do. Some unknown power was pushing him to it. He forgot the vow, forgot his father's fate. Wonderment, beyond his power to resist, drove him on. His father had said, and so had his mother, that the spirit of the *waddan* attracts, stupefies, robs a man of his mind, takes all his will away. Then the hunter finds himself dispossessed, led away, haunted, leaping on his own four limbs as he chases the beast over the smooth, hard rocks.

What made him forget the sacred vow that day, leading him to pursue the *waddan* in such utter surrender, like one in the grip of some fierce passion, passed all understanding. A mighty secret lives in this animal, one not found in the magical gazelle. "I fear the *waddan*," his father had said. And he was right. Hadn't his end come at the *waddan*'s hands?

God! What but sheer madness was thrusting him on now, to aim this noose toward the horns of the mighty *waddan*? What secret power was leading him to entangle the great beast's head, and so bind their fates together? Had this too been long since written on the tablet of destiny, written before he was ever formed in his mother's belly and born into this harsh world? What was this ecstasy? Was it the fervor spurred on by songs and music and the beating of Sufi drums in the oases, of which his father had told him?

But the blind rocks knew how to waken him from these passions. The second the rope closed on those awesome horns, the great beast leaped furiously in the air and sped toward the slopes strewn with their harsh stones. He dragged Asouf over the ground, crossing the wadi with an agility remarkable in a beast of such size. His father had been right. "When the *waddan* takes flight," he'd said, "he'll carry you off toward the most merciless rocks, toward the worst parts of the mountain." He was racing toward the slopes now, toward the rugged part where jagged rocks stuck out like the fangs of wild beasts. The mountain's the *waddan*'s refuge, his fortress. His safety. Still Asouf clung on to the rope, while the *waddan* shook his head in jerky movements, trying to free himself, yet speeding on toward the stony heights. Together they reached the slope armed with its black rocks. Asouf tried to get a grip on one of these, but had to let go. A moment later he was in front of another jutting stone, which he grasped with his left hand, his right still holding on to the rope. The crazed beast was pulling in one direction, Asouf gripping the stone to hold him back. He felt his arm about to be ripped from his shoulder, but he summoned his strength, refusing to let go of the stone. Then, in the twinkling of an eye, the stone was pulled from the earth and the *waddan* went on, dragging man and stone behind. Asouf only noticed the stone when they'd gone on still further, into the kingdom no one knew as he did. He let the stone go, feeling, for the first time, a burning sensation. His whole body was aflame with burns, his skin torn with the wounds made by the stone.

His face was covered with sweat. What covered his knees, and legs, and hands, and elbows, was blood. His clothes, already tearing as the battle began in the wadi, were now being ripped to shreds by the stones and bushes on their way to the *waddan*'s stronghold on the mountain tops.

Still the *waddan* leaped on, over jutting stones and rocks. Asouf was seized by terror as he saw the size of the boulders coming now. Should he let go of the rope? Abandon it? But how could he retreat after this savage fight? How could he surrender after his blood had been spilled, his body gashed by the stones? How could he return home and face his mother, covered in wounds, caked with blood, defeated and empty-handed? How could a hunter soil his hands with blood, then return without his prize?

A bigger stone lay right in his path, and he hugged it in his left arm. Now, he thought, we'll see which of us two's the stronger. Who was stronger? A young man killing a furious beast, or a *waddan* breaking the rocks with his horns? There are legendary desert stories of the *waddan*'s strength. Still he hugged the black, smooth, burning rock, and still, without halt, the stubborn *waddan* pulled at the rope, with violent, jerky leaps. Now Asouf's right arm was about to be ripped off. He tried to summon help from his bloodied legs, burning with their wounds, but the great beast gave him no room for maneuver, the leaps growing ever more frantic, tearing and cutting Asouf's limbs. He let out a scream, a scream whose echoes rang through the mountains like the shrieks of the jinn. He could endure no longer. This *waddan* was in the prime of his vigor.

Asouf had, finally, to resort to cunning. Patience and cunning. Only through patience and cunning, his father had said, was a proper life possible. War, too, could be won only through patience and cunning. What is life but a war? And he was waging it now. If the *waddan* didn't tire, if Asouf didn't drive him to exhaustion at last, then everything had been in vain. And the beast was in its full vitality and strength. Asouf let go his hold on the rock, with a sense of numbness and relief and despair all together. He cursed himself for doing it.

The chase went on. Only it wasn't a chase. Rather a kind of dragging and scraping along the ground. On they went, up the steep, jagged slope. He began to lose the feeling of pain from the wounds, and the warm blood flowing from his hands and feet and body began to cool and clot. When pain becomes unbearable, the body starts to lose all sense of it. The limbs were numbing, and pain was eating up pain. Pain lessens pain.

The *waddan* began climbing the most rugged rocks of all. Asouf closed his eyes, so as not to have to see their ugliness and huge size. Suddenly he was standing up on his feet, still bound to his victim-executioner, and he leaped behind him, thrusting his torn body backward. He ran behind him with legs wide apart, clashing with the stones, striking against the rocks, and there he was at last on the top of the mountain. Briefly the *waddan* ran straight toward the edge of the abyss on the other side. Oh, God! What was he trying to do? Where was he going to drag him? Into the pit? The *waddan* leaped toward the worst part of the unknown chasm. Asouf heard the horns of the savage beast crash against a rock. Then, a moment later, after a single brief moment like a flash of lightning, he found himself hanging from a jagged rock on the top of the mountain, his legs dangling into the everlasting pit. How and when he released his hold on the ill-fated rope he never knew, or what destiny led him to this rock to which he clung. Catching his breath, he looked down, trying to make out the bottom of the chasm. But he saw nothing but darkness. His heart beat on, his lungs panted on. How had this happened? He was desperately thirsty, his throat and mouth dry and parched. His limbs were bleeding freely. The heat was unrelenting, though it was already late afternoon and the sun had begun its slide toward sunset. It beat down remorselessly on his bare head—he had no veil now. His turban had been snatched off, in the first moments of the conflict, by the bushes in the wadi. He waited for his breath to grow more even, then looked right and left to examine the spot, seeking some way to safety. He tried to swing his feet onto the top, but stones tumbled down on his head, and he was afraid to repeat the attempt for fear of falling into the abyss. He looked below, his feet searching for a rock or a hollow onto which he could leap to save himself, and saw a crazy rock overhanging the pitch blackness of the pit, as though suspended from the sky. He moved his trembling hands from their hold above his head, inching to the left, examining the hanging rock above. But it was smooth, with no possible handhold. He moved back to the right in slow, cautious movements—but there was just a smooth edge rising upward. Again, nowhere to find a hold. He was the prisoner of two feet of ground, as if in a grave. Was this his grave then? Was it the end? He wept in his fear. No sound came out, but a liquid hot as embers burst from his eyes and burned his cheeks. Was it really fear, or was it rage? Rage at the defeat, or because his greed and betrayal of the vow had led him into this trap? The vow! He remembered it now. His father had died too because he'd betrayed the vow. Was he going to die then? Did death come so easily? Was it so near it needed only a moment of exhaustion, in which he'd loosen the grip of his fingers and plummet down into the chasm? And was life so very short? Why had his father or mother never told him death was this simple, life this short, that a moment's foolishness could lead you to the abyss? Only sheer foolishness could have made him take on that possessed *waddan* and loop the rope around his horns. What else had that moment been?

And was this what people called fate? His father and mother never tired of repeating the word, and only now did he understand its meaning. Fate—the hidden secret that conjures up a *waddan* to tempt to the bottomless pit. His hands could bear his weight no longer, and exhaustion was taking hold. His lack of movement was bringing pain back, his hands and feet were raging with it. He'd known, from his struggles with camels, that exhaustion always came later. A wound only really starts to hurt when the blood's dried. But he mustn't give in to pain. The battle wasn't over yet. It was only just starting, over the mouth of the pit, in the very heart of the stillness. If he gave up now, he'd be lost. But what was he to do about thirst? How could he endure that, hung between earth and heaven? His throat was dry, his lips parched, without spittle. He tried vainly to make some spittle. Dryness had pierced deep into his throat, down into his stomach. He'd lost every drop of moisture in the battle. It had come out in the beads of sweat. But he must wet his dry throat. He must catch a drop of moisture to bathe his cracked throat.

Forcing out his tongue, he licked the tears flowing over his lips. They tasted salty, but that was better than having his heart burst. He loosened his right hand and began to lick it, to lick the still flowing blood. Salty and sticky. Then he held on once more with his right hand and began licking the blood from his left. He went on between the two, resting each for a few moments at a time.

In front of his face floated the shadows of a passing cloud, images of thirst and exhaustion. Soon he'd tumble into the pit. He'd fall sooner or later, so why go on? How much longer was he to resist, hanging from a stone like a bat? What was he waiting for? Who was there to give him water? Who'd come and rescue him from this trap? His mother was an old woman who couldn't leave her home among the caves. His father was dead and the world was a desert. The man who chooses to live free in the desert must look after himself. Such was the philosophy he'd read in the life of his father, and his father had paid for it with his life. Now he too was to pay the price. Was that what freedom meant? Was living apart from people a crime to be settled by death? Was solitude a denial of God?

Why was he torturing himself? His fate was sealed, and no miracle was going to save him, any more than it had saved his father before him. There are no miracles in the desert. If you fall into the trap, you have to get out alone; and, if you can't, you have to face your destiny with courage. So, why not simply let his hands loosen themselves from this rock for one tiny second, let everything end for ever? He only had to let his fingers unclasp, or stop moving his hands as they took turns on the means of safety, on this small jagged rock. He'd plunge down, and his heart would burst before he reached the bottom of the abyss. He wouldn't suffer. There'd be no pain.

Pain was here, on the rock, clutching on. Pain was in life. The jutting rock was life. How cruel life was!

Where was his courage, his nobility? The fear of committing a shameful act? Where were those things his father had spent his whole life striving to plant in his heart? He'd consider himself alive, he'd said, so long as those principles were alive in his son's heart. Only when his son betrayed any of these things would he himself die. And so, his father was undying even in death. No, he wouldn't betray any of these things. If life was so easy to renounce, why did God give us life at all? Life. The eternal desert, ever sad; the happy, leaping goats and the graceful fleeting gazelles; the murmurs of the mother in the cave on winter nights. That was life. How could he abandon it, loosen his clutch and leave it, to plummet into the abyss?

10. THE SECRET WORD

He wouldn't give up the jutting rock, wouldn't loosen his fingers. Patience. He'd almost forgotten the wise advice his father had passed on! "I tell you. Be patient. How can you live in the desert without patience? The man who was never granted its contentment will never be happy there. I tell you. Use patience and cunning, they're the secrets of the desert. No one can know where succor will come from, whether from heaven or earth. Above all, be patient and wait. Patience is the secret word."

Evening came and darkness took hold. He tried repeatedly to swallow, but there was no spittle. His strength was quite used up, his arms growing slow and heavy in their movement. He gathered all his strength into his hands. He gathered the hidden strength the desert, over all those years, had planted in his heart. A man's strength isn't in his body. It's in his heart. As evening fell, he began to resist with his heart.

His heart granted him wakefulness. He opened his drooping eyes and sucked more blood from the wounds on his arms. When there was nothing left to suck, he bit into his hands with his teeth to suck more blood and moisture. The darkness and silence were crueler than the chasm.

He listened to the silence, trying to hear the jinn speaking together. Where were those good jinn, who loved, at other times, to talk so loudly together? Why didn't they come and save him? Or at least keep him company, and banish this desolation in the blackness of the pit? You concourse of jinn, he thought, where are you? But the jinn gave no answer, not even the smallest murmur. They didn't come that night.

The goats had run off. They'd go back to their home in the caves, if wolves didn't strike them down first. The poor old woman. What would happen when she saw the herd return without him? She'd die of fear. Oh, God, if he should die, she'd die too. Why hadn't he thought of that before? His mind had been utterly confused. But now the strength of his heart brought clear sight, to see he was in a state crueler and more hateful than death. His mother would be on her own now, until the day she was finally devoured by wolves. She'd never survive without him. She too would pay the price of solitude. The price of freedom. The price of living apart from people and their malice. There, among people, was malice and humiliation; here, in the desert, was freedom and death. That was why she'd quarreled so constantly with his father, taunting him for not mixing with others. She'd always known the matter would end badly, but her only weapon had been tearful protest. And now there she'd be alone, weeping in the cave, waiting for death. No. No, he wouldn't die. He wouldn't let himself die. He must do something to save himself from his plight. He moved his feet, striving with all his heart's strength to reach the top of the ledge with his feet. He swung them above his head, but the stones and mud rolled down on him, threatening to rip off the ledge itself. In despair he brought his feet back down. He loosened the grip of his right hand, and it dangled in the air, stiff and hard like a palm branch.

He took a deep breath. The jinn. Oh, you concourse of good jinn, where are you? The man not granted patience had no place in the desert. But where would succor come from, even if he were to stay here in this trap for a thousand years? God's desert was vast, and this place wasn't on the path of caravans or a place of pasture for herdsmen. And even if the miracle should happen, even if God decided to send someone to try and save him, where would he find him in this hidden spot over the bottomless pit? No hope of succor. No hope. He heard his father's voice: "You must be patient even when you've lost hope. That's the law of the desert." Then, without any conscious will, he found himself shattering the depths of the silence with a horrified scream, the scream of despair. "Ah! Ah! Aaaaah!"

The mountain peaks, huddled in silence and darkness, sent back his screams, still louder: "Ah! Ah! Aaaaah!"

The echo rang on, endlessly. But the jinn made no response. As for humans, he'd no hope his screams would bring help from them. There were no human beings here. There'd been none for a long time. From the moment his father had left this world, turning toward the everlasting void, he'd sought nothing from them—only to avert their evil and escape their harm. Was this the punishment for those who lose all converse with the human race?

He was growing weary, his strength quite ebbing away. He drew strength from the heart, and licked the wounds on his arms, the dried threads of blood. Patience, patience! He felt dizzy, his consciousness about to fail. A kind of cloud was passing before his eyes. He shook his head to rid himself of it, with the help of further screams.

"Ah! Ah! Aaaaah!"

Again the mountains rang, still louder this time.

"Ah! Ah! Aaaaah!"

Then silence took over once more. No whisper, no movement. Not a murmur. And no jinn—there weren't any, it seemed, on mountain peaks. Where were the jinn?

He fought drowsiness and the phantoms of fatigue. Images floated before him, tempting him to slacken his grip on the loop of consciousness. If he should faint, he'd drop into the abyss. He must keep thinking of the fate of his poor mother, after his death.

What could the old woman do in that wilderness? She'd die of thirst or hunger, or the wolves would devour her. He mustn't die. He had no right to die and leave her to face such a cruel fate. He was a wrongdoer. He'd broken his vow and he'd earned his punishment. But what had she done, that she should deserve to die with his death? Where was the justice? Where was God? When he'd reached seven years old, and begun to learn the *Fatiha* chapter, his father had asked him:

"Do you know where God is?"

He'd pointed his finger upward, and said: "In heaven."

His father had roared with laughter at that.

"God's here," he'd said, pointing toward his breast. "Not in heaven!" Then he'd murmured, as if to himself: "In the heart. With us, in us."

He'd raised his eyes toward Asouf with a strange look, as if he'd returned, after a long absence, from a journey to some distant country. Then he'd whispered: "If anyone asks you, just say He's in the heart. Remember that always. In the heart."

Asouf hadn't understood the words then. How could God, the Great One, the Mighty, All-Powerful One, lodge in this small heart, be imprisoned within the cage of this chest of his? Now, hanging from the top of the cliff, he realized his dead father had been right. Where was he finding all his strength to endure, if not from the heart? But for this mysterious strength, but for the presence of God in the heart, he'd have fallen into the abyss of darkness that was plucking him down by his feet.

During the second half of the night, he imagined he'd fallen asleep while still hanging there. How was it he hadn't fallen? Perhaps it was a delusion. Perhaps he'd never fallen asleep at all. His pain returned worse than it had ever been before. He couldn't go on, he couldn't endure. There was no hope. No hope. Where was the heart's strength? Where was God? Soon he'd plunge in. He lost the power to move his hands, could no longer change them as they clung there to the rock. It was all over, no hope of deliverance remained. And no hope of deliverance for his mother either. Wretchedness had been written as her lot, and she'd suffer for a long time before she died. That was the worst thing—that she'd suffer before she died. He let out a deathly scream, the rattle of a choking man in the very throes of death. The sound filled him with fear, increasing his despair.

He began to loosen the grip of his clenched right hand on the ledge. Soon it would all end: pain, thirst, and the anguish at his lone mother's fate. Everything would vanish. The eternal desert would disappear. He wouldn't see the gazelles any more. He wouldn't see the mirage dancing on the horizon. How cruel, that the desert should disappear! How could he bear it, parting with the desert? The worst thing, after his mother's suffering, was never again to see the eternal desert merging into the vastness of God. Then—he heard the sound of footsteps, above his head. Was this one of death's delusions? A dying person sees what others don't see, hears what others don't hear. Slow steps—cautious, hesitant.

The sound of footsteps rolling the stones as they moved on. Was it possible? Could the miracle happen? No, impossible! These were the phantoms of a dying man. Just opposite him the horizon split in two, to reveal a thread of light, the light of early dawn. There was silence for a few moments. Again he listened, hoping to hear the illusory steps. Illusion or not, they'd planted hope in his heart. He opened his eyes, and couldn't believe it. Something rough touched the fingers of his stiffened hands, as they clutched there on the life-giving ledge. Something rough. Was it a rope? Holding his breath, he opened his dead fingers, clutched this thing, the rope, the rough hemp rope. Still unable to believe it, he held on with both hands, clung to it. He'd never, ever leave it. He'd cling on even if they burned his hands with fire. The rope pulled him, his head was looking over the top. He couldn't make out anything in the dark. A body was moving there in front of him, pulling him powerfully. Was it the jinn? Still the body moved there, dragging him away from the mouth of the abyss. His chest touched the ledge, and he felt how all the mountains that had pressed on his chest had gone away at once, tumbling into the darkness of that wild, hateful abyss. He was saved. Saved! The jinni who'd saved his life was still moving in the stone-covered space, slowly, silently, calmly. He tried to make it out in the darkness of early dawn. He closed his eyes, then opened them again, a number of times, then focused at last on the patient phantom. He saw some of its features. Oh, God! It was the *waddan*! The same *waddan*. His victim and executioner. But which of them was the victim, which the executioner? Which of them was human, which animal?

The mighty *waddan* was still now. He saw him raise that great head, crowned with the legendary horns, and face the mysterious thread that heralded dawn. The faint, divine glow within which the secret of life forever dwells anew. Suddenly, in the dimness of the glow, he saw his father in the eyes of the great, patient *waddan*. The sad, benevolent eyes of his father, who'd never understood why man should harm his brother man, who'd fled to the desert, choosing to die alone in the mountains rather than return to men. The eyes that had chosen a cruel freedom without ever quite knowing why.

From his place, covered with its greedy stones, he cried out in a choked voice, as if communing with his God.

"You're my father. I recognized you. Wait. I want to tell you—"

He lost consciousness.

11. THE WARAN

He woke with the twilight. The sun had scorched him and he'd recovered from his faint. The desert sun can wake the very dead. For all the fierceness of its morning rays, it was lost in mist and darkness now, a veil screening things from him, like a dust storm. Was it the wind? Then he remembered his thirst. The thirst that sets a veil on everything. He tried to move, but the pain returned. With a mighty effort, he forced his limbs to move, crawling over the peak, taking care to avoid the abyss. He couldn't have missed that if he'd been blind! He'd never in his life forget where it was, his heart would warn him if he walked blindfold. But for the heart, he would never have escaped it.

He found a suitable place and began his descent, holding on to the rocks. But his foot slipped, and he tumbled down, so far he thought it would never end. The stones tore at his limbs, but they were deadened already and gave him no pain. He surrendered to the slope, and at last found himself holding on to the bushes of the wadi. He tried to open his eyes and examine his arms and legs, but the hazy screen only grew thicker; then it covered the world with darkness.

He fainted once more, and at some time the sun woke him

once more. Stretching out his hand, he plucked some dry leaves from a wild bush, then crawled on along the wadi. He remembered patience. But for patience he would have fallen into the pit. He made one more mighty effort, summoning the last strength left in his heart, and crawled on, along the length of the wadi.

It was desperate progress, a final move. Movement now decided life or death, spurred on by the resolution of a man in the grip of death to take in one last draft of life, even if his head should be sliced from his body. A goat breathes, takes in air, long after it's slaughtered. Even when its head's cut clean from its body. As for a slain *waddan*, it gets up, headless, and runs off a long way, before giving in at last and submitting to God.

Then there's the waran. With that things are even worse. You kill it in the morning, then, when you fling it on the fire to grill it at night, it leaps from the blaze and runs right off.

There's another life, between life and death. A third state neither void nor existence. He was in that state now, crawling along the wadi like a snake, his eyes blinded. He could see nothing, feel nothing; he was just seeking the drop of water he'd left yesterday down in the bottom of the wadi before the battle began.

With a trembling hand he felt the canvas wrapped around the canteen. He drank. Then he slept. He woke again at night, the second he'd spent away from his mother.

12. The Transformation

He wanders the wild forests
Among the caves and crags
Like a moufflon exhausted
With sorrows, seeking
To flee what is ordained
In the eternal tablet
But fate's dispensation
Flies forever about his head.
—Sophocles, *Oedipus Rex*

After this he felt an aversion to meat, to meat of all kinds. He noticed the change first when a small kid died and he found his mother cooking it in the cauldron at the mouth of the cave. He'd returned from herding, and the smell assailed him from far off. He felt dizzy and nauseous, and retched repeatedly before finally arriving home.

Meat aroused his disgust now. He was astonished he'd once been able to enjoy it. How could one creature eat the flesh of another? What was the difference between the flesh of an animal and that of man? If someone could eat the flesh of the *waddan*, then he could eat human flesh too. Had his father come to dwell in the *waddan*, and the *waddan* in his father? He, his father, and the mighty *waddan* were one now. Nothing could separate them.

All this irritated his mother, who said it was the work of the jinn and urged him to seek help from a magician's talisman.

"Be a man, won't you?" she scolded angrily. "Have the merchants from the caravans bring you an amulet from Kano or Timbuktu."

But he didn't deign to speak to the merchants on the subject. He wasn't afraid of the jinn, nor had he any wish to seek protection against the *waddan*. Who seeks protection against himself? But he didn't tell her the secret—the secret of his transformation.

13. The Journey of the Body

The people in the oases wove many myths around the transformation.

He was driven from the desert by drought, and had, for the first time in his life, to go down to the oases and venture his lot among people. His "pilgrimage" to Ghat happened just as Captain Bordello was launching his campaign to seize the young men of the oases and force them into the camp he'd prepared, to train them for the invasion of Abyssinia.[vii]

Before that drought came, the sky had drenched the desert wadis with floods. These floods had taken them by surprise, driving the old mother from the cave, and he'd found her remains three days later in Abrahoh. Stones had torn away her limbs as she was swept on and on. Her head was disfigured, and the bushes had plucked the short silver hair from her small head, leaving it almost naked; nothing was there on the skull but a few scattered hairs caked with mud. The right eye had gone, ripped away by the stones on that savage journey, and an empty, gaping space was left. The other eye was shining, staring up at the sky. With the head he found part of the neck covered with a layer of mud, which had dried over the blood. The arms and legs, and the rest of the body, he'd found scattered along the length of the wadi, torn apart, over those three days, as if hacked by a knife. The right hand was still clinging on to the thorns of an acacia, as it had been before it was ripped from her body, and on the arm the bones shone through in several places. The merciless stone had eaten up the soft parts. He tried to wrench the thorns from the crazy grasp, but in vain; the flesh had all fallen away, but the bony fingers still clung on stubbornly. She must have gripped the tree as the waters swept her away, and still held firmly to the thorns. But the frenzied might of the flood overcame the mad desire to keep hold of life and breath. Then the body had been severed from the arm, which was fixed fast to the thorns of deliverance. The thorns of life! Here was that third state, between life and death, being and void, heaven and earth, which he'd seen in slain animals, which he'd known himself as he crawled along the wadi in search of a drop of water. Between life and death was a space from which a creature could return to life, or else cross over into death, go on into the void and darkness.

He couldn't, there in the long, broad wadi, find the other remains. Whenever he found a piece of her body, he'd place it in his bag, climb up to the heights and bury it there, so that his martyred mother had five graves along the tops of the wadi, each far from the other. The memorial stones stood like signposts, condemning the unknown transgressor.

ᴖ

14. The Two Opposites

The flood had set on them with its old, immemorial
weapon—treachery. He'd seen no sign of it coming. The
sky had been clear since morning, quite bare of clouds, and
this had led him to go out early with his goats. At night, too,
he'd noticed no lightning, heard no remote rumbling of
thunder. But Tadrart and the whole Akasus mountain range
were seeing streaming night rains, heavier than for many long
years. And, as usual, the wadis didn't gush with the flood for
two days more. The torrent had taken his mother by surprise,
at dusk, while he was away in the pastures.

Man in the desert had to die by one of those two
opposites: flood or thirst.

After her death, he spent some weeks on the heights with
the goats he had left, until the rushing waters abated and the
thirsty wadis began to absorb them. Thousands of years of
thirst had caused the land to do away with the rivers. It had
become dry and cracked, parched for water.

That year the wadis and plains, and the fringes of the
mountains, became thick with forests and plants and grasses.
He saw trees he'd never seen before, ate herbs he'd never
eaten. Where, he wondered, had the desert hidden the seeds

for these plants? No sooner had the rains poured, the waters flowed to every corner, than the cruel, gloomy, drought-stricken land had turned green with plants of a thousand kinds. They simply sprang up, and the dull, dried-up trees turned green in a few days. It was as though the seeds strewn in nothingness, in the folds of the sands, among the massive rocks, had been waiting for that moment, eager for the sky to meet the earth. And when that consummation came, the seed buried in nothingness quivered and breathed out its relief, cracking earth and stone alike, stretching out its head in search of sun and life.

It pleased him to stoop down and contemplate the small leaves that had cracked the layer of mud and raised their heads from the void, impelled as they were by the force of life. They'd ripped through the veil of darkness to find joy in the open spaces. Water grants life to the desert, just as it had granted death to his old mother.

And, as usual, the surging floods were followed by drought. This drought was long, lasting more than four years. In the first and second years he lived on the plants the generous floods had provided. But in the third year the south wind, blowing over the desert in waves, destroyed what trees remained and sucked the last hope of life from the wadis' plants.

In that third year the herd of goats began to perish too. All he'd nurtured during the year of plenty, kids and goats, was wiped out by that south wind. The wadis all turned yellow, became wilted and desolate. The goats, finding nothing else to eat, searched for dung among the rocks, eating their own droppings from the years of flood.

Asouf would sit on a rock above the well, pour a little water for them to drink, and gaze at their bodies, withered and scrawny, listless and gaunt. Where was the robust spirit that marked goats out? The energy and mischief? That natural vitality of the kids? Where were those strong he-goats endlessly butting one other, fighting over some beloved she-goat? Where was the clever gaze, from the black and luminous eye?

All this had vanished. The goats couldn't, at last, find any cakes of dung redolent of the grasses of that strange year. Even the merchants from the caravans were no longer willing to barter. Once he'd gone and tethered three beasts up on the heights, then withdrawn some way off and waited for the caravan to pass on its way to Kano. The merchants had arrived, taken a close look at the she-goats, talked among themselves, then gone off without leaving him anything. They'd rejected the goods—his goats were no longer fit for exchange. What was he to do? How would he live without dates, and without barley?

But that disaster was easier to bear than the one that followed. The herd began to die off. One morning he rose at dawn to find a she-goat had perished during the night. Then two more she-goats followed, and a he-goat and a kid. Then the corpses became regular.

He grew ever more anxious, and began to think seriously of going down to the oases. The decision wasn't an easy one, but he could see death creeping closer by the day. The wadi was strewn with the bodies of goats. He'd watch them die, not even moving to slaughter them; for, since what had happened there at the pit, he no longer butchered or ate meat. He'd be woken at night by the noise of wolves fighting over the stinking carcasses. Then, in the morning, he'd heap sand over the rotting corpses, with their bellies and entrails torn by the wolves, their eyes, so black and sad and beautiful before, eaten out by maggots. Even so, he didn't leave the caves for the distant Akasus mountains until the last goat had died. Then the final thread with Massak Satfat was cut.

Jᒎ

15 INTO THE FIRE

Captain Bordello's men seized him the day he entered the
oasis. Finding him sitting against the wall in the
ironmongers' market, trying to catch his breath after the long
trip, they manacled his hands and led him off to the Italian
garrison on the hill. Inside he found a group of young men
similarly taken, who laughed as they saw him coming,
exchanged mocking remarks, then started bombarding him
with questions. When they learned he'd just come down to
Ghat from Massak Satfat, remote and afflicted with drought,
one of them laughed uneasily. "That's what you call coming out
of the frying pan," he said, "into the fire." They all laughed.

Next morning they were packed together like sheep, in a
long line, and led off toward Uwaynat, en route for Marzouq.
There the crazed Captain was waiting to train them, then use
them to fulfill his heroic dreams of invading Abyssinia from
the east with troops on camel back.

On the way something happened—something the people of
the oasis constantly recounted, around which they wove
legends. The young men told them how they'd witnessed a
miracle for the first time in their lives. They'd seen a man
break loose from his captivity and change into a *waddan*, then

run off toward the mountains, bounding over the rocks like the wind, heedless of the bullets flying all around him. Had anyone ever seen a man transformed into a *waddan*? Had anyone ever seen a person escape the Italians' guns, running on until he vanished into the darkness of the mountains?

The wise oasis Sufis, enraptured, rocked their heads from side to side and threw incense into the fire, convinced one and all that this man was a saint of God. That evening they went to the Sufi mosque and celebrated a *dhikr*[viii] through the night in praise of God and in homage to the saint, filled with joy that the divine spirit should have come to dwell in a wretched creature of this world.

That was Asouf's first and last encounter with the oasis people. He went to Massak Mallat, where he tended his herd of camels. And there God opened for him a door He'd open only to his saints: a passing cloud crossed the lower wadis, and they flowed with water. For several months he stayed there in the sandy desert, with his camels, until the depths of the sky at last took pity on the mountain desert and he returned to the caves of Matkhandoush.

Had the Sufi dervishes, in their vision of the holiness of God's spirit incarnate, read the secrets of the unknown?

16. Prayer

Cain insisted Asouf should go with them in search of *waddan* in the nearby mountains, seating him between the two of them while Masoud drove the truck. Wiping the sweat from his brow, he cursed the desert with vile words Asouf hadn't heard before—he'd never in his life heard such ugly expressions. What had the desert done to deserve all these insults? The truck sped on, eating up the plain that merged into the horizon.

This was the second time Asouf had ridden in a truck. The first time had been with the white-haired Italian expert, who'd seated him next to himself in a land rover and asked him to point out the caves of the Wadi Aynesis. He'd scoured the surrounding mountains with him, rock by rock, setting up stones near some of the caves and sprinkling a white liquid on them to mark them out from the rest, then returned with him to Matkhandoush. The Italian had given him some cans of food, a loaf of bread, and a packet of biscuits, then, with a smile, he'd gotten into his Land Rover and driven off eastward to Abrahoh. He was a good, friendly Christian. On their way back they'd encountered a pair of *waddan*, a male and a female, running slowly toward the mountain. The female was pregnant, and the male had to hold back to match her slow, heavy progress. The Christian had a loaded rifle on the back seat, and his hand stretched behind him, his eyes still following the pair as they moved among the craggy rocks. Asouf thought for a moment the man was going to take the rifle and fire at them. Beads of sweat broke out on his forehead, and an odd shudder swept through him. But the Christian just picked up a pair of binoculars and put them to his eyes, watching the beasts until they vanished among the shadows of the high mountain. This Christian, he thought, remembering his treatment at the hands of Captain Bordello's soldiers in Ghat three years before, wasn't like the others.

Had he thought that because the Christian hadn't killed the *waddan*? Or because he'd given him some cans of food and other gifts? No, it was neither of those. It was because he'd sensed how this old, white-haired man loved the desert. He'd seen it in his eyes, and in the way he treated the painted rocks. He saw how the man's fingers trembled when they touched the caves marked with the lines the ancient people had made. As he did it, a mysterious glint would appear in his eyes. He'd take his handkerchief from his pocket and rub the dust from the faces painted on the hard rocks until the picture was completely revealed. Then he'd step back a few paces and gaze at the image, his lips parted in a smile perhaps, but his eyes filled with the shadow of sadness. Sometimes he'd stand there for a long time, in front of the painting, his hands folded on his chest, inclining his head to the right and the left, in his eyes a humble submission like that of a Muslim when he prays. He'd utter words in a foreign language, quite wrapped up in himself. Then, coming out of his trance, he'd smile apologetically and pat Asouf on the shoulders, as if to reassure him he hadn't gone mad!

They'd crossed the plain now, and Massak Satfat was becoming visible. The heights, covered with their huge black rocks, burned in the sun's everlasting fire. The peaceful sandy desert, stretched out flat and merciful to God's worshippers, ended, and the mountain desert began, angry and inhospitable, its face set sternly against the wanderer. The rancor was, it seemed, a legacy of those remote times when unending battle was waged between the two harsh deserts, a fiery enmity even the gods in the upper sky had never contrived to soften or reconcile. And here the mountain desert was now, eyeing with hatred these visitors coming from its old rival. The truck bumped, jerked repeatedly into the air, and Masoud had to bring the speed right down. The great rocks forced him to swerve and dodge, so as to stay on the narrow tracks and avoiding tumbling into unforeseen gulfs and hollows.

Asouf had warned them against the surprises and base deceptions of the mountain desert. The ground would seem a flat expanse, then suddenly a pit would be there in front of you. Wadis clove the earth, looking like mere fissures, but they went plunging down. Each time Asouf gave warning of a chasm or hidden wadi, Cain would exclaim: "He's a jinni, didn't I tell you? Who else but the jinn would see these traps? Without you we'd have been down in one of these wadis long ago!"

The sun moved slowly from its throne, a hint of defeat appearing on it as it moved toward sunset. The sun always has a sad, dejected look when it begins to slide down, perhaps because it's bidding farewell to the desert on its daily way to its chamber. In the morning those signs never appear on its face. It looks cruel and frightening then, threatening creatures with torment and pain.

The truck veered down, across the slope, into a deep wadi.

Asouf had all the while been praying and reciting the *Fatiha*, begging God not to let them see a *waddan* as they went along. The moment they reached the wadi, Cain told the driver to stop the truck. He got out and started searching about.

"Aren't these *waddan* tracks?" he said.

Asouf got out after him.

"I don't think so," he said, in a faltering tone. "They look like goat tracks."

"Goat tracks?" Cain said, staring at him suspiciously. "You're telling me these are goat tracks?"

The stare remained fixed on Asouf, and there was anger and veiled threat in it. He walked on, following the tracks of the herd, and repeating: "Goat tracks? You're telling me these are goat tracks?"

Then what Asouf had been fearing all day happened. From behind a rock, just opposite him, a *waddan* peered out, following their movements in the wadi. Asouf quickly turned away, thanking God Cain and Masoud hadn't noticed the mighty animal. In an effort to hide his confusion and distract their attention, he raised his head and began his afternoon prayer with a loud "God is great!" He sensed the animal was still there behind him, watching them from the hollow in the rock. The poor beast had scented his presence and felt safe from the guests—for the *waddan* had begun to trust him now, grazing close to him in large herds. Ever since he'd stopped eating meat. Since what had happened there at the pit, since he'd seen his father in the eyes of that great *waddan* who'd saved him from death, then quietly approached him before he lost consciousness. The herds came to him in the pastures, mixed with the goats. The males came right up to him and snuffled his clothes, gazed at him with meek, mysterious eyes that conversed in a thousand languages, spoke with a thousand tongues, without making so much as a sound, then went off to graze among the thickets. At the start he'd been struck dumb, paralyzed with amazement. With time, though, he'd grown used to them, and begun playing and speaking with them, recounting stories to them, telling them of his worries and problems: of the harshness of the desert, his fear of mixing with people. And they'd console him with those eyes of theirs, which conversed in a thousand languages, spoke with a thousand tongues, without ever making a sound.

This *waddan* knew him now, and wanted to greet him. He'd fall into the hands of people whose only food was the meat of gazelles and *waddan*. Careful! Go, quick! Leap into the heart of the mountain, you mountain spirit! Back to your redoubtable secret stronghold. Tell your fortress to swallow you up until the danger's past.

He finished his prayer. He once more besought the mountain, silently, to save its spirit. He looked behind him. The *waddan* had disappeared.

At that moment, Cain bent over some *waddan* droppings, took them in the palm of his hand and said angrily: "Are these goat tracks too?"

17. THE FOUNDLING

This business of meat dated from his very infancy. His father had died from a knife wound while his mother was still carrying him, the mother herself from a snake bite when he was just a week old. His aunt, his mother's sister, had stepped in to take care of him, and on one of her trips to the Hamada, on the advice of a religious teacher, she'd given him gazelle's blood to drink. This, he'd told her, was the only way the ill omen could be averted and the rest of his family and relatives be protected from the curse that had pursued him from the moment of his conception. But the aunt and her husband both perished from thirst during the trip, and a passing caravan picked up the nursling infant as he was thrusting his head into the open belly of a gazelle, licking at the blood and dung. This blood, it was said, was what had saved him from the fate of his aunt and her husband. Had the head of the caravan known the child's history, he would never have picked him up. He had no notion this "little angel" was to bring about his own downfall and cause his trade to fail.

Desert bandits seized his herd and plundered his caravan on its way to Timbuktu. The robbers fell on him right at noon, as he was enjoying an afternoon sleep in the safe middle oases.

They would have overwhelmed him but for a loyal assistant who rushed to his aid, frightening off the assailants with an old Ottoman rifle they hadn't had to use before on all their trips. The man had never supposed the day would come when he needed its help among the peaceful people living there! But if the merchant's life was saved by a miracle, the robbers seized the wealth he was carrying with him across the great desert.

Only when he found his adopted son eating raw meat from a plate, the blood dripping from his teeth, did he understand the true reason for the disaster. On one of his next journeys to Kano he consulted a soothsayer, who told him to bring a hair from the infant's head or a piece of his clothing. The man took a leather bracelet from his wrist and handed it to the soothsayer, telling him it had been around the child's neck. The soothsayer moved his head from side to side, gazed up toward the heavens and uttered his spells. Then he threw the leather bracelet into the fire, murmured for some time in Hausa, and finally, his eyes reddened, said quietly: "The one weaned on gazelle's blood will never know the straight path until, as a man, he has his fill of the flesh of Adam."

It so happened Adam was the merchant's own name. Astonished, he cried out to the black soothsayer: "Have his fill of my own flesh, you mean?"

The magician remained unperturbed. "From Adam, I said," he went on. "I didn't say from your own flesh."

The merchant stormed out of the man's hut, and, two days later, went to consult the most famous soothsayer in the place, telling him the whole story of the foundling, from the beginning up to the moment he'd seen him eating the raw meat. The soothsayer asked for time to consider. When the merchant returned at the appointed hour, he was stunned by the answer.

"Cain, son of Adam," the soothsayer intoned, "you will never have your fill of meat, or of blood, until you eat from Adam's flesh and drink from Adam's blood." This he repeated three times. Then, after much talk, he agreed to write a protective amulet.

But even the talismans of Kano soothsayers have no power against what's written. The amulet was lost during a trip, and the boy went back to ripping at raw meat with his teeth. As for Adam, he made a trading expedition to a tropical region, where Yamyam tribesmen, famous for their love of pale meat, tore him to pieces and ate his raw flesh.

18. The Cannibals

Cain became notorious for his love of uncooked meat, until finally his playmates started calling him "son of Yamyam." When he quarreled with neighboring children, they'd taunt him with it.

"You!" they'd cry. "You ate your own parents! You'll eat all the meat in the world, you devilish son of Yamyam!"

At that he'd hurl himself on them, and they'd run away. He'd show his teeth to frighten them, then start grinding them like the Yamyam, until they finally yelled and ran off home, pale with terror. He did it as a joke, but he couldn't see his face as he did it, and didn't realize how much like a cannibal he looked!

He didn't give up this horrifying habit, not even when he'd grown up and become the most famous hunter in the Red Hamada. Whenever the craving for gazelle meat came on him, he'd wake in terror, then wake his companions too, so they could all go off hunting together. Masoud, who'd gone with him and been with him more than anyone else, liked to tell of the strange time Cain decided to give up eating meat. After a month, his whole face had changed and grown pale, his body began to droop, his cheeks started jutting out, and he suffered from headaches and nervous seizures. Sometimes a violent shudder would pass through him, his lips would be covered with foam, and he'd drop to the ground, convulsing furiously like a slaughtered chicken. Masoud would rush to sprinkle water on him, then fetch him a cup of green tea— tea, he believed, could cure any addiction, even an addiction to meat. Perhaps this was because addiction to green tea was the only sort known in the desert. But it was all in vain, as Masoud finally realized the night he was woken by his friend's weeping and lamentation.

"I can't," he was crying. "I can't, I tell you. I can't take it any more!"

And so Masoud had gone off with him to hunt a gazelle, which Cain had eaten that same night.

In those years the Hamada had teemed with life, and there were herds of gazelles everywhere. The rains were generous, never holding back for long. If the sky should be dry and miserly with water one year, the next year its yearning for the earth would save the seeds from damage and death, and protect the wild bushes and trees from drying right out, so that deliverance always came. The plains would turn green in the spring, the birds and rabbits and gazelles would flourish—if you chanced, suddenly, to look over the upper plains, you'd be greeted by the sight of the most beautiful of creatures peacefully grazing. The moment they sensed the movement of humans, they'd up and flee, and, as they ran off all together, the whole plain would seem to move. Yes, the very desert seemed to be flying human attack.

There was another reason, too, for the abundance of gazelles then. Neither Land Rovers nor rapid firing guns had yet arrived to disturb the desert's peace. The merciless vehicles arrived with the companies searching for oil and underground wealth. Then, a few years later, came the invention of the devilish weapon specially designed to violate the Hamada and destroy the peaceful herds. One of these, given him by the officer of the American camp in Gharyan, was Cain's pride and joy.

He'd come to know this officer when he was still hunting with the old Ottoman rifle inherited from his adopted father, when he'd head for the open spaces on camel back in the company of his childhood companion Masoud. When spring came, they'd leave the sleepy town on the edge of the western mountain and spend long weeks away, only returning when their food and water was exhausted. With them they'd have stocks of dried gazelle meat, and they'd go to the camp to seek out the American officer, who'd buy Cain's surplus from him, or else exchange it for sacks of flour, or for tea, sugar, and canned food.

After they'd known one another for three years, this officer taught him to drive and presented him with an old Land Rover, so he could pursue the lovely creature in earnest. Only when he came to own this amazing, devilish machine, and could see the beast from close quarters while still alive, was he able to note its remarkable beauty. Before that no gazelle would let him come closer than two hundred yards. The gazelle's the most sensitive and watchful of all the desert animals. It scents humans from far off, and is only seen close up with the sudden onset of dawn or dusk, or on days when the wind drops and the air's totally still.

Now, though, the jinni wheels gave Cain the chance to gaze his fill at this loveliest of creatures. Masoud would take over the wheel, and they'd cut through the herd, carefully picking out their victim. It was usually Cain who made the choice. Then the driver would fix his sights on chasing it through the wide expanses, which stretched out toward the horizon as though they'd never end. On the gazelle would fly, and the devilish machine would pursue it, catch up with it, run alongside. There was the gazelle you'd dreamed, as all desert children do, of holding in your hands. You'd dreamed of stroking his graceful neck, touching his golden hair, looking into his sad, intelligent eyes, kissing him on the forehead and clutching him to your heart. In this beast was the magic of a woman and the innocence of a child, the resolution of a man and the nobility of a horseman, the shyness of a maiden, the gracefulness of a bird, and the secret of the broad expanses.

And there he was now, exhausted, broken, sweat soaking his body, his lips covered with foam. He could endure no longer, and yet still he endured, endured adversity. His manner of running is quite unlike any other animal's. He doesn't, as the *waddan* does, seek out the rugged mountain terrain. He doesn't swerve in circles, doesn't dart this way and that. He races straight on, through the open spaces, disdaining the ignobility, the shame of breaching the rules of racing. He chooses heroism before the shifts of cunning, rejects trickery and craft, keeps firmly to the path of chivalry. Poor gazelle! He doesn't see how this devilish machine is a betrayal of nature, breaching the rules of noble conflict and seeking to win the day through the ugliest trickery.

Cain had little thought for the rules of nature. His concern was to hunt just as many gazelles as he could, and so quench the flames between his teeth and calm his belly, then sell the rest to the American officer at the camp.

19. The Migration

And then this American, John Parker, presented Cain with a further devilish machine. With the introduction of rapid firing guns to the desert, the gazelles' chance of escape was far less, and the herds virtually died out. How well he remembered the rivers of blood he spilled after getting his hands on that gun! Down he'd go to the plain, teeming with its gazelles, and start gathering in the harvest. A single round would bring down several beasts. He'd press the trigger once more, and again the gazelles would drop, like clusters of dates torn apart in a storm.

This storm struck at the unborn too. In one raid a bullet pierced the belly of a pregnant gazelle, who took shelter in a small thorn bush, a whimper of pain passing her lips. She let her unborn calf drop, then began licking the blood and mucus from the small creature's body. The gazelle was bleeding, and the wounded calf was bleeding too, trying to lift up its head that the bullet had pierced. When it lay quite still, and the mother realized it was dead, she lifted her own head to the clear sky in a scream of pain, a tragic scream. As she turned her head back, Cain saw great tears in her eyes. She took two steps toward the truck, then fell down dead, those mysterious eyes gazing into space, eloquent with their wretchedness.

Before that he'd hunted one gazelle in a raid, two if he was lucky. Now the situation was reversed. He could slaughter the whole herd in a single raid, with just one or two gazelles escaping if luck smiled on them. As the number of slain animals grew, so did the amount of meat he ate. He'd breakfast on one gazelle, lunch on another and have a third for his supper, with still one more if he happened to have a guest, some passing herdsman, perhaps, or a merchant from a caravan. He never dreamed that one day the gazelles would become so scarce, never dreamed this beast, with which the desert had once abounded, could ever die out. Only then did he remember the small unborn calves he'd taken from slain gazelles—especially that gazelle whose calf he'd killed in her belly, and who'd complained to heaven against him. But he forgot all that soon enough, still scouring the Hamada in search of the fleeting herds, who'd retreated southward now, seeking refuge in the heights of the Hasawna mountains.[ix]

Wayfarers and caravan merchants told how they'd seen gazelles crossing the frontier into the Tassili in long, hard marches, traversing regions carpeted with those fearful black stones. There were, they went on, traces of blood everywhere where the stones had torn their share of the booty, ripping savagely at the hooves of the migrating herds.

The Hasawna mountains became a temporary fortress for the gazelles, as they sought safety there in the Algerian desert, using the formidable mountain chain as a refuge to recover from their wounds. Then, when they were healed, they dashed off again on their long road, toward the far south. For the old hunters, this strange transformation, never witnessed by the desert in all its history, was a sign from heaven. The wise among them sought God's special protection each time they prayed, invoking His aid against the evil of man and the greed of the son of Adam, which had led to this devilish weapon and threatened to wipe out the most beautiful of creatures, forcing such herds as remained to migrate to the ends of the earth—not for pasture but in a quest to survive and save their young from death.

These hunters would meet in the naked wild and sit around their green Chinese tea, talking and consoling one another. "The gazelle's like the *waddan* now," they'd say "It's seeking out the mountain tops. Surely the end of time has come." No one sees into things as desert people do, no one can match them in reading the secrets of the unknown. Whenever they meet, they seek some means to interpret the signs of time.

20. Only through Dust Will the Son of Adam be Filled

Help, Lord; for the godly man ceaseth; for the faithful fail from among the children of men.
—Psalms, 12:1

And the Lord God said unto the serpent, Because thou hast done this, thou art cursed above all cattle, and above every beast of the field; upon thy belly shalt thou go, and dust shalt thou eat all the days of thy life.
—Genesis, 3:14

The quarrel flared up suddenly. When they were back from their exploration, Asouf made a comment about Cain's gross appetite.

"I heard my father say," he remarked, "that only through dust will the son of Adam be filled."

If only they'd been successful in their quest, Cain wouldn't have become inflamed by this. Now, though, he turned furiously on the bedouin.

"What do you mean by that?" he yelled. "Eh, goatherd?"

"All I said," he repeated simply, "was what my father told me once. Only through dust will the son of Adam be filled."

"Are you trying to make fun of me, you cursed old fool?" Cain shouted.

Masoud roared with laughter at this, but his companion silenced him with an evil look, then turned back to Asouf. As he approached, the bedouin began fleeing toward the cave where his herd of goats was hidden. But, swiftly though he moved, Cain caught up with him and blocked his path.

"You'll regret this, by God," he screamed, "you cursed old fool! Do you think I'm a complete idiot? You play the innocent, claim to live like some sort of hermit, and all the time you know exactly where the *waddan*'s hiding out! Do you think I don't see right through you?"

Asouf started trembling, and a cold sweat broke out on his back. Cain shook his fist right in Asouf's face, until it actually touched his turban.

"If you don't show us where the *waddan* is, you'll regret it, believe me! I'll make you see stars, and at midday too. I mean it!"

Masoud moved up, but Cain motioned him away without even looking at him. Asouf retreated a few steps more, fluttering his hands as if about to take flight. He had no idea what to do.

Cain's eyes bulged, and his mouth became flecked with foam. His madness was mounting.

"Masoud," he yelled, "fetch me the rope." He returned to Asouf. "Two days now you've been laughing at us, as if we were children. Now it's our turn to laugh at you, you son of a bitch."

The herdsman was rooted to the spot, unable to move even his long arms. He stayed frozen while Masoud brought a rope, a long hemp rope. Cain went on with his litany of accusation.

"Aren't you ashamed of yourself? An old man like you, telling all these lies? They told us in the oases—you're the one person who knows where to find the *waddan* around here."

Asouf opened his mouth, but found nothing to say in reply. Stupidly, he repeated the saying yet again: "Only through dust will the son of Adam be filled!"

Cain went for him first, but Masoud followed. To their astonishment the bedouin put up no resistance.

"You won't get away from me," Cain said, "the way you escaped from Captain Bordello's soldiers. The people told me all about that, but I don't believe you changed into a *waddan*. Do you hear me? I don't believe you're a saint."

He finished tying Asouf's wrists and feet, then stood there with his hands on his hips. His black gun was clearly visible.

"If you really are a saint," he roared, "the way they say, then fling off those ropes and run off to the mountains the way the *waddan* does. Ha, ha, ha! If you do turn into a *waddan*, then I'll eat you straight off. Ha, ha!"

But Asouf only repeated his saying, the way someone might repeat a protective spell in the face of the executioner: "Only through dust will the son of Adam be filled."

At that Cain lost all vestige of control. Stung by Asouf's apparent defiance, he went for his bound victim and started dragging him along the sandy wadi, toward the tall rock where the splendid mythical *waddan* stood alongside the High Priest. Then he stopped, exhausted, wiping the sweat from his brow with his arm. He shouted to his companion.

"Are you just there to watch? Why don't you come and help me?"

Masoud went up and helped him drag Asouf to the rock, holding him by his right foot, while Asouf looked at him with eyes that were frightened and pleading. But the man paid no attention to his silent entreaty. Perhaps he didn't even notice it.

Cain walked around the tall rock, then climbed it from the back where the ascent was easier, where a line of caves stretched to the southwest down into the bottom of the wadi. He peered toward the sheer side, then shouted to Masoud.

"Get me the rope. Throw me the end of it."

Masoud whirled the hemp rope through the air, and Cain, trying to catch it, lost his balance and almost tumbled down. Then, at the last moment, he clung on to the ledge. He stayed motionless for a time, then, more furious than ever, he repeated as if to himself: "Come on, you cursed old fool. Show me your magic. Put on your *waddan* skin and run off to the mountains. Where's your magic, you saint of God? You slave of slaves?"

He gave a powerful upward tug on the rope, and the rock scraped against Asouf's back. He let out a groan. Cain fixed the noose on to the high ledge, while Masoud played his part, pushing the bedouin's body upward by his bound feet. Asouf groaned once more. Cain looked at the hanging body, but, not liking the position, climbed down and ran to the truck, returning with another rope. He climbed the rock once more, from the same gentle side with its line of caves, and tied the new rope to the right wrist, fixing it to a ledge on the right-hand side of the rock. Then he produced a knife from his pocket, cut the old bond with his knife, and tied the right foot with the new rope, on the right side, parallel to the arm. He returned to the left foot, tying this firmly with the rope, then stretched it away from the other by fixing it to a ledge some way off. Asouf was crucified now, his legs and arms wide apart. His body covered the majestic, legendary *waddan*, while the priest's hand touched his head now bare of its turban, as though patting it.

His white-flecked beard and balding head were visible now. There was astonishment in his eyes, ambiguity on the face of the priest: The priest's mask became ever more inscrutable.

Cain's tone was menacing.

"Come on, speak up! Where do we find the *waddan*, you

slave of slaves?"

And Asouf, with a kind of childish insistence, answered with his talismanic spell: "Only through dust will the son of Adam be filled!"

~~

21. THE COVENANT

The last caravan left, and one lone gazelle, followed by her small calf, continued to wander the Hasawna mountains. This gazelle was trusting to an amulet inherited from her mother, designed to guard her against the evil of man.

Along with her calf she grazed, in the darkness of early dawn, in the plains alongside the blue mountains, taking refuge among the rocks the moment the breath of morning came and the horizon was streaked with light. All day long she sheltered in the shadow of those impregnable rocks, moving among the slabs burned by the rays of the arrogant sun, springing onto the tops of the rocks as the awesome *waddan* did, so as to amuse her calf and compete with it in grace and play and running, until the last of the other gazelles had joined the long night journey.

The wise gazelle, seeing the loneliness in the eyes of her little one, told her just why she was venturing to linger behind, rather than go along with the migrating herds. But before telling her more of the protective magic, she decided one evening, by way of warning example, to relate the story of their homeland. She told how, when the Creator made the soul, He assigned for it three frontiers and set it within three prisons: time, place, and the body. Any who attempted to break free from these was justly cursed and consigned to perdition, since the Creator had hallowed them and made them a destiny for every creature. Any attempt to pass beyond them was disobedience to His will.

Now, it so happened that one gazelle, made vainglorious by its great horns, abandoned the herd on the plain. It climbed high into the mountains and scaled the highest peak—that awesome blue summit, turbaned in mist, that even the *waddan* fears to approach. And what was its punishment for this disobedience? The Creator sent a wild bird for which no summit is too high, and the bird ripped open the gazelle's belly with one blow from its claws, killing it and sending it tumbling down the slope, back to the plains. He who seeks, she went on, to leave his appointed place has sought to leave his body. He who seeks to leave his body has sought to leave time. He who seeks to leave time has laid claim to immortality. And he who lays claim to immortality blasphemes against his fate, presuming to be above the miracle of creation, to compete with the divine. And he who competes with the divine is consigned to perdition. So why (she concluded) should they flee their fate and move on to the Tassili? How could they leave the Hamada plains, with their unlooked-for gifts, their flowers and grasses and truffles and breezes, and migrate beyond the sands to where serpents creep and wild beasts roam?

Here, her calf ventured an objection. The beasts the Hamada had seen, she said, over the past few years, were wilder, fiercer, and crueler than the very beasts of the jungle. The mother nodded in agreement, then turned aside to relate the story of the protective magic handed down to her by her own mother. It was a talisman unmatched throughout the desert, the like of which no other gazelle had ever possessed. Without it she would never have found the courage to remain there in the heart of the mountains, knowing as she did of the curse destined to follow all migrating beasts who violated one of the three principles on which the law of creatures was built. There was no life for a migrant in alien lands, for the curse of heaven would find him wherever he went. The only talisman able to protect against beasts and evil ones was patience in calamity.

"Once," she went on, "in a spring long ago, a wandering traveler lighted on a plain covered with new grasses. He crawled among the bushes, on hands and knees, leaving his family up on the heights. We heard a baby screaming in the lap of a woman who was swaying, trying to fight back weakness, barely able to stand on her feet. This, my wise mother said, was because of thirst. A migrating family had found itself alone with the arrogant sun, and the sun was afflicting them. As the nursling baby raised its voice in complaint, the mother tried to calm and console it with low murmurs, while the man, on hands and knees, continued to crawl toward us. I stayed close to my mother, begging her to let us flee. I was terrified, I admit it. It was the first time I'd ever seen a human so close, and in such a wretched state too, his lips flecked with foam, his face covered with dust. His features were haggard, his lips chapped. He was utterly weary as he struggled on, striving to catch his breath and open his dimmed eyes to gaze at us. They were frightening, those eyes, as though staring into emptiness. The poor man had no weapon. If he'd been armed, he would surely never have had to act as he did, in a way we couldn't believe as he appeared there on the plain. The herd watched him curiously. All the older beasts were gazing at the sight, all sad on his account.

Various discussions broke out, then the oldest gazelle addressed us.

"'God,' she said, 'honored all creatures and gave them life. Then, to test their endurance, He set them in the desert. He placed His secret in the scarce water, and He placed a further secret in dreadful sacrifice. He who sacrifices himself to save another's life sees into that secret and wins immortality. A son of men is about to die of thirst. Nothing can save him but blood.'

"Here a pitiless gazelle broke in.

"'The sons of men,' this gazelle objected, 'are evil and murderous. Have you forgotten, honored mother, how they spilled the blood of so many scores of our tribe in that fearful slaughter? How can we sacrifice ourselves for an accursed butcher?'

"The gaunt old mother smiled. 'Sacrifice,' she went on, sadly and patiently, 'knows nothing of bargains, and doesn't look to the soul for which the sacrifice is made. Sacrifice belongs to the Almighty Creator. And don't you see, my good fellow gazelles, that nursling angel lying in the woman's arms? He's committed no crime, had part in no slaughter.'

"'Don't be taken in by that,' a mean-spirited gazelle shouted. 'He may look innocent now. Wait until he's older and kills scores of beasts from our herd!'

"The mother rebuked him, then announced she was going to offer herself as a sacrifice for the son of Adam. Cries of protest arose, and the din grew ever higher. I looked toward the poor human, and saw how, utterly worn with fatigue, he'd plunged his head and hands in the sand. Then I saw my mother leap to the wise mother's side.

"'We won't,' she cried out to the herd, 'permit our honored mother to offer herself as a sacrifice. We'd lose our guiding

THE BLEEDING OF THE STONE

light, who's led us along the true path. Besides, see how gaunt and withered she is, without a drop of blood in her body. Look at her, you good beasts! Is there any blood there at all, one drop to save a family? With our good mother's agreement, I propose to go in her place.'

"Shouts of praise arose. Then the honored mother turned to my own.

"'This,' she said, 'is a further secret of sacrifice. And it will make a covenant between your progeny and the sons of men. The blood of your daughter, and of your daughter's children's children, is forbidden to him for all eternity. This is the covenant, the immutable pact and the bond of blood, and a curse will fall on any venturing to betray this bond. Through all the earth there is nothing stronger than the bond of blood, and no crime more hateful than its betrayal.'

"At that my mother came up to me, kissed me and rubbed my neck. 'I'm doing this for your sake,' she whispered. 'From today on, man will never touch you.' Then she went and gave herself up to the broken man, his face covered with dust beneath the thorn bush. I didn't understand what followed then. My young mind wouldn't let me take in the cruelty of it all, and I had no sense of danger until I saw the knife shining in the human's hand, beneath the sun's rays. If only you could know, my little one, the pain that tore at me then! I felt as though a poisoned arrow had pierced my heart. I screamed, I ran straight at the honored mother and struck her with my horns that were beginning to appear, crying out that she was an old jinni. Then I leaped toward my mother, around whom the whole human family had now gathered. The woman approached and placed her thirsty baby in the belly of my poor mother, who was already slain.

"The human chased me off. I don't know why he didn't

plunge the knife in my neck too. I went back to the herd and climbed the hill opposite, raising my complaint to heaven against every creature—against humans and gazelles, against the honored mother. I asked heaven to curse them all for the pain they'd caused me, and, whenever I remembered my slain mother, I felt the poisoned arrow pierce my heart once more. My poor mother! She did it for my sake and yours, so our progeny would enjoy safety through all the generations. Her blood made a bond of brotherhood between our kind and humankind. We and humankind, I say, are brothers now. And this bond of safety was bought with cruel blood."

The wise gazelle, her story completed, rose, then gazed up toward the summit, as if invoking some talisman in the heavens. Darkness still lay over the eastern plains, but dawn had begun to streak the horizon with light, its threads weaving a blue veil around the heights of the mountain peak.

~

22. THE OPIUM

John Parker, a captain at the Hweilis Base, had been chosen to run a subsidiary camp, set in a strategic spot on the Naffousa mountain. In his student days he'd studied Zoroastrian, Buddhist, and Islamic Sufi thought at the University of California, and he'd kept his fondness for eastern philosophies. Upon joining the Marines and moving to North Africa in 1957, he'd seized the chance to plunge himself into a study of Sufi ways. When they'd landed in Tunisia on the way to Tripoli, he'd left his comrades (who'd gone to spend the evening in a bar), choosing instead to visit a *dhikr* circle. Although it was strictly against Marine rules to visit "doubtful" places of religion, the embassy official had seen no harm in meeting his wish, and together they'd gone to witness the rituals of dervishes chanting and ecstatically invoking God's name. It had, though, been a wretched experience. When they'd been standing by for just a few minutes, some young boys began throwing stones at them, driving them out of the circle. He'd returned to his ship with a fair number of bruises to show. His drunken comrades had made fun of him, telling him it was an old eastern tradition for curious strangers to be stoned.

IBRAHIM AL-KONI

What fascinated him above all was an idea advanced by a French writer: that it was the Maghreb that had brought Sufism down from its throne of heavenly philosophy, to the common soil of everyday life. Here in these countries, in contrast to the Arab east, there seemed no difference between the wise sage, the simple dervish, and the pious saint—they all looked like wandering beggars! And so Sufism here, as an esoteric philosophy, was actually closer to Buddhism. There was no difference between God in heaven and the poor vagabond on earth, so long as God Himself was prepared to take up His abode in such holy fools.

In the same book he'd found the thrilling text that led to his passion for gazelle meat. The author had quoted a passage from an obscure Sufi traveler, who'd written as follows: "The truth lies in grazing beasts. In gazelles God has placed the secret and sown the meaning. For him who tastes the flesh of this creature, all impotence in the soul will be swept away, the veil of separation will be rent, and he will see God as He truly is."

This mystical passage would never have evoked such an echo in him had he not been interested, too, in the Buddhists' bold ideas on dumb animals. When at university, he'd repeated to Caroline an inscrutable passage from Zen teaching, to which he was deeply attached in those days. Man's search for union with God could, it said, only be realized when he'd passed through the animal state. He must live apart until he became an animal himself, silencing his tongue until he lost the ability of speech, eating grass until he forgot the taste of food. The Creator was more inclined to enter a creature living deep in the wilderness, secluded even from those animals that seek the company of humans.

He'd said many things of this sort to Caroline (who'd been infatuated with him), but he'd very stupidly failed to acknowledge he'd taken them from Buddhist teachings. As a result she'd supposed he was crazy and left him!

The obscure Sufi text brought him back to these outlandish notions, which had shattered his first relationship with a woman. Now he decided to use his isolation, here in the western mountain, to try to unravel the secret: to taste the flesh of this legendary animal, in the hope that God would open the door to him, that he'd know the bliss of seeing Him as He truly was. He was surprised by the Sufis' agreement that grazing creatures were specially worthy to receive God's holiness and presence, but he saw a strong parallel with Zen teachings, which set a greater value on animals than on man. They too had preferred some animals to others, placing savage beasts beyond the pale of mercy and ascribing holiness to those that were peaceful. The obscure Sufi took his vision still further, listing numerous strange illnesses whose only known cure was the eating of gazelle flesh. He needed gazelles, he told people—and right away they told him about Cain the son of Adam.

"If disaster ever struck," they said, "and all the gazelles in the desert perished except one, then Cain would find it and eat it up." They told tales, too, of Cain's legendary passion and greed for the meat. A dervish expressed it in cryptic fashion. "There's a worm in this creature's mouth," he said, "that makes him eat his very self if he finds no meat to eat." This dervish was a solitary old man who sat each day with his back against the wall of the mosque, facing the rays of the twilight sun. He didn't mix with others, and people avoided him because of his odd ideas on religion and the world. Although the general at the Tripoli headquarters had warned against mixing with local people, Parker couldn't resist the temptation, and he spoke with the old man everyone accused of being an outlandish dervish and heretic—he was shunned, apparently, because he'd fallen out with the other Sufi shaykhs. Once, when the two had gone together to a *dhikr* session, where dervishes tore at their faces and breasts, and brandished knives in the fire of their passion, the old man had led Parker right away.

"Look at those Tijani heretics!" he'd said. "Look at the heresies they're contriving, the way they're wrecking Sufism and Islam!"

On the way back, John had asked, suddenly: "According to your order, does God dwell in gazelles?"

The old man had been silent for some time. Then he'd said, as if talking to himself: "God dwells in all souls. To limit it to gazelles is heresy."

He'd turned to John and added: "That's one of the Tijani heresies."

Parker had read of the controversies between North African Sufis. This dervish, he'd learned already, belonged to the Qadiri order—which was why the Tijani shaykhs incited people against him, and he'd become an outcast. The man produced further surprising ideas that evening, as he went on talking about God's incarnation in earthly beings.

"That's our difference with you people," he said. "With you Christians. You say Christ is God, limiting God's glory to one creature, while we see Him present in all creatures. Our religion's more just than yours."

The wise dervish urged him, too, to change his view of the Sufi ways of life. The deeper he went in his quest, the man added, the more vitally important the things he was likely to discover. This Qadiri Sufi taught him many secret things. And as he came to know Cain better, and Cain went on supplying him with gazelle meat, he discovered that the dervish, like the Buddhists of Tibet and the Himalayas, ate no meat at all, but lived on barley bread. One day, even so, the old man made a passing reference to the *waddan*. He told him, in that mysterious tone he used when about to impart some secret knowledge known to no one else: "Take oil from Gharyan, dates from Fezzan. And meat? The *waddan*." He laughed. "Oh," he went on, "if the Tijani heretics only knew I was revealing the secrets of the desert to Christians! They'd stone me!" He gazed at him for some time, then went on in the same tone: "The *waddan*'s truly remarkable. I tasted it in the old days, when I used to eat meat. The divine secret's in the *waddan*."

He remembered this exchange when Cain, coming and telling him how the gazelles had died out in the desert, asked for the use of a helicopter to scour the Hasawna mountains.

"There've been some stray gazelles sighted there," he said. "The Hasawna mountains are the gazelles' last stronghold."

"It's not allowed to fly search helicopters over the desert," Parker said. "You know that as well as I do. The rules are clear enough."

"If a man wants roses," Cain said, "he'll put up with their thorns. Do you know that saying?"

Parker laughed.

"If a man wants roses," he repeated, "he'll put up with their thorns. Well, that's true enough. I don't know which of us loves roses more. Me—or the creature whose teeth are eaten by worms and can't live a single day without meat!"

Cain laughed in his turn, but the joke struck home even so.

"We've done with gazelles," he said, red-faced, but managing to hide his anger. "It's the *waddan*'s turn now."

"The *waddan*!"

Cain sipped his tea in silence. Then he said: "The *waddan*'s difficult to hunt. It hides away deep in the mountains, down in the southern desert. A journey there takes preparation, fleets of vehicles, specialists. And you won't give me one helicopter to search the Hasawna mountains. If a man wants roses, he'll put up with their thorns. The thorns of the *waddan* are stronger than gazelles'!"

"I wonder if either of us could put up with them!" John retorted. "You can't stand the desert thorns, I know. You'd like to reap the fruits without the sun and the dust. You'd like to hunt gazelles in silk gloves." He laughed sarcastically. "You don't love the desert," he went on. "Shaykh Jallouli, the one the other shaykhs in your town call a heretic dervish, says water cleanses the body and the desert cleanses the soul. I've never come across anyone here who's more faithful to the desert—and yet he doesn't savor its bounty the way you do. He doesn't eat its gazelles. You, Cain, eat the fruit and curse what produces it. The desert hasn't cleansed you, because you've never truly loved it. And now you demand whole fleets of vehicles to take you off in search of the *waddan* down in the southern deserts. You want to blackmail me the way you did with the gazelles all those years. You're not just selfish and greedy. You're lazy too."

Again Cain held himself in. He simply smiled. "If I wiped out the gazelles," he said evenly, "you helped me do it. You gave me the trucks and the guns, and you ate your fair share of the bag—more than your fair share. You're the one who wiped out the desert gazelles, after hammering my ear with all those fairy tales about the poor beast's meat having divine secrets lurking in it. You're the biggest criminal of the lot. You say how marvelous gazelles are, how innocent they are, then you sink your teeth in their flesh, in search of some secret that doesn't even exist outside your own weird head. You pretend to be kind to animals, and yet you're greedier than me, greedier than all the meat eaters in the desert. The worm tickling your teeth's fiercer than the one in mine."

But there was no other way of reaching the Hasawna mountains and combing it for the gazelles the wandering herdsmen said they'd seen. They flew off in the helicopter, on a secret mission Shaykh Jallouli anointed with curses. Ever since hearing of the slaughter of the gazelles, he'd refused to have anything to do with Parker. First he stopped shaking hands with him and returning his greetings, then he started sending people to him with warnings and curses. One Friday the two came suddenly face to face by the old souk. Jallouli lowered his head and tried to move on, but Parker wouldn't let him.

"How can you claim," the *shaykh* murmured then, pain in his eyes, "to belong to the religion of Christ? You're no part of him. You've nothing to do with him, or he with you."

With that he wrapped his cloak around his head and disappeared into the crowd. Parker never saw him again, but he couldn't forget the look of pain in the man's eyes as he'd uttered those harsh words. Only then did he sense the hateful crime he'd committed against one of the loveliest of creatures. But what could he do? Gazelle meat was like an opium. Once a man tasted it, he got used to it; and once he'd got used to it, he'd go mad without it!

23. FLESH OF THE KINDRED

Twilight. The mountain peak loomed on the horizon, still wrapped around in its blue mask. As the day advanced, and the sun grew more arrogant, the haze became fainter, turning to sky blue. This was the only peak in the desert to wear a sky blue mask.

Early morning, there in the broad expanses, likes to weave this blue around the mountain, holding it apart from changes in the desert's mood. Cain sat next to the pilot, while John sat behind, alongside Masoud. The pilot was a black man with a large nose. He looked sullen, his features severe, but all this vanished the moment he smiled, for his mouth was studded with marvelous white teeth, and his laugh was captivating. When he burst out laughing, it was difficult for him to stop, even when Captain Parker reprimanded him or prodded him with his elegant stick.

The legendary Grasshopper hovered in the clear sky over the silent, empty Hamada plains. In the wilderness below grew ratina, lotus, and acacia, mostly scattered, but bunched thickly in wadis that had seen plenty of recent rain. There were grasses, too, clinging to the dried up beds, still green in some places, and signs of plentiful water on the slopes, though less on the uplands.

The birds had migrated north. On the whole trip they met just one, flying high in the sky, gliding through the space and steadily beating its wings in the manner of one resolved to cross great distances. This was a migrant too. Everything abandons the desert as summer draws near, leaving the wilderness to struggle with mirage and silence, and with the sun's rays.

They didn't see a gazelle all the while. The gazelles hadn't gone north, like the birds, but south. Cain peered out of the Grasshopper's window and pointed to a fissured wound, about to heal, in the dark gray land.

"See that?" he said. "That's where the gazelles passed through."

The thin thread, on the harsh landscape strewn with black stones, led them on to the Hasawna mountains. The great Grasshopper veered around their eastern edge, then flew southward alongside them. Now the gray desert appeared, stretched out as far as the eye could see. Down in the depths of the sands they saw the tops of palm trees, bunched together, knocking one against another, as if whispering secret spells designed to ward off the dust storms.

Here the Hamada ended. And here began the great sea of sand, everlasting stay of the pathless wilds. It was in this wilderness that creatures hid away, fleeing the butchery of humans.

The Grasshopper wheeled around in a wide circle, keeping close to the slopes of the range, and hovered on, at a low altitude, until midday. The mirage rivers overflowed, threatening, it seemed, to sweep away the mountain feet.

John Parker began to despair. As for Cain, he was bored, the hot sweat stinging his temples. John shouted, over the roar of the engine: "No sign of your gazelles here. They're not in the Hasawna mountains."

"But the herdsmen saw them," Cain yelled back. His tone was one of frustration. "Just a few days back. Where did they run off to, in all this sand?"

The sky-blue turban had vanished from the peak, which was stark and bare now.

"We'd better go back," John shouted.

A depressed silence hung over them, while the Grasshopper's devilish propeller went on whirling like a mill. On it wandered, over the slopes of the range, seeking out hollows and rocks and naked slopes, until it looked, from a distance, like an eagle in relentless search of prey.

They landed at the foot of the mountain, then searched for some shelter to protect them against the malevolent sun. The shady caverns were up on the heights, and the way to them was over rocks, smooth and broad, but topped with stones like the fangs of beasts. Wild grass clung on between the stones, surrounded, here and there, by smooth tongues of sand, bearing the traces of snakes and lizards and desert rats.

And Cain discovered other tracks too—of gazelles. Had it been a herd, or the gazelles the herdsmen had spoken of? He hopped about among the rocks, then came back down the mountain like one bewitched.

"Gazelles," he shouted. "Gazelles! Back to the helicopter!"

The group rushed to the Grasshopper.

"They're new tracks," Cain went on, panting. "I found droppings too. They're hiding up somewhere around here."

He stood near the plane, wiping the sweat off his face, panting from fatigue and high excitement together. Then he saw her, standing in the shade of a large crag on the right-hand side of the slope, where a narrow path split the rocks and descended into the wadi. Her eyes were big and black and intelligent, speaking some unknown language, saying something to him, revealing a secret. A secret, yes, one he sensed but couldn't quite grasp. It's the hardest, most desolate thing in the world, to sense a secret and not grasp it. What was this beautiful creature trying to say?

He looked back at her. She didn't move. Alongside stood her calf, gazing at him too, with an enigmatic look. She too was speaking, agreeing with what her mother had said. How hard it was, not to know the language of such beasts. He felt awe, and fear too. He didn't even notice Masoud tugging at his sleeve, drawing him away. The black pilot was laughing, showing all his splendid teeth.

"My God!" he was saying. "What's he hanging about for?"

Cain sank down into his seat. The sweat was pouring from him even faster, and he was breathing hard. John was talking, and so was Masoud. All three were talking, making various comments. Apparently they hadn't seen what had happened, hadn't noticed the encounter between Cain and the gazelle. The helicopter took off.

But Cain was still deep in thought. He'd fought gazelles and hunted them for as long as he could remember. But he'd never before seen a human in a gazelle's body. He was amazed he hadn't fired at her. He'd forgotten all about his gun, forgotten he'd come on a hunting trip. He'd forgotten he was Cain, son of Adam, born to love meat and blood. How could he, Cain, have held back from pressing the trigger, when a graceful gazelle stood there in front of him? Had she really been a gazelle at all? And was he really Cain?

The helicopter hovered in the sky, deliberately low, following the mountain chain westward.

"Well," Masoud remarked, "now we've seen gazelles living peacefully in the mountains."

No one answered. He had to continue himself. "According to the sages, that's a sign of doomsday."

The air was moving now, the beads of sweat cooling. But the mood of despondency remained. John ventured on an answer to Masoud's comment.

"Your *shaykhs*," he said, "look at every natural phenomenon and see a divine sign pointing somewhere or other."

Masoud laughed.

"You're right," he said. "If their visions had turned out right, we'd have had doomsday a thousand times over at least."

Then, gazing at John, he added slyly: "Your Sufi *shaykh* friends know that well enough too."

"Jallouli doesn't talk like that, though," John answered. "He's never said anything to me about signs of doomsday."

"Because he's worldly. That's why he's fallen out with the *shaykhs* from the other orders."

"Maybe it's the other way around. Perhaps they're the worldly ones, and he's the so-called apostate who's decided to be different. Jallouli's pious and virtuous."

"Well, if a Christian says so, that's enough to damn him as a heretic."

"Is that your idea, or just what the *shaykhs* from the other orders think?"

Masoud laughed.

"Maybe it's what I think too."

"Well, there's no escaping people's malice."

"That's one of his own little sayings, isn't it?" Masoud was laughing again. "I reckon he's pretty clever. He can even put Christians through the hoops. The other *shaykhs* don't realize how dangerous he is!"

Cain took no part in all this. As for the jolly black pilot, his laughter kept ringing out, even though he couldn't follow the exchange.

They'd reached the end of the mountain chain now, and John instructed his pilot to turn and fly back the way they'd come. The helicopter veered in a wide circle, then they flew back over the wadi before, finally, the pilot wheeled around once more toward the mountain.

Again they examined the harsh carpet of stones. John turned to Cain.

"I don't know," he said jokingly, "what Cain's going to do with that worm in his teeth. It's the fiercest worm known to man."

Cain grasped the opening.

"Well, there's no sign of gazelles," he said. "Let's go back."

Suddenly the pilot cried out.

"Look. Look there!"

The mother gazelle's soft coat shone from afar, then she vanished as quickly as she'd appeared. The pilot flew toward it, hovering over the dark cranny where she was lurking, at the mouth of the opening, trying to protect her small calf with her body. She was trembling.

The Grasshopper hovered right over the entrance to the crack. The pilot shouted: "Fire!"

Masoud and John followed suit, yelling in unison: "Fire!"

Cain was trembling, like the gazelle. He pointed his gun toward the crack, and their eyes met. He turned his face away, closed his eyes, then pressed the trigger. The blast of the gun sounded. He wiped the sweat that was pouring now over his face and wrists. The noise the others were making, drowning even the roar of the engine, hammered in his ears.

He looked toward the crack, and saw the small calf writhing on the ground, while her mother stood over her, bleeding heavily herself, licking the blood from her slain baby's body. Then, suddenly, she sprang and crashed her head savagely against the rocky opening. The look in her eyes had changed completely. Was it wretchedness?

She leaped toward the open, lifting her head to the clear sky rent by the sun's rays, then she howled, tragically, in the way hungry wolves do. It was the first time they'd heard a gazelle howling like a wolf.

Then she dropped to the ground and lay on her right side, craning her head toward the *qibla*. The frightening expression hadn't left her eyes. Cain couldn't approach, but the rest ran toward her. A knife glittered in Masoud's hand.

That night, Cain, son of Adam, didn't just kill his sister. He ate her flesh too.

24. THE AMULETS

It was the only time Cain had tasted *waddan* meat. Caravan merchants had brought a slab from Agades, and his neighbor had given him a large dried piece. He'd torn a piece from it there and then, leaving the rest for the dinner he'd arranged with Masoud and John Parker that Friday evening in the Wadi Sidr, where their oasis bordered the Hamada from the south and west.

He sent word to his divorced wife, by a local lad, to prepare the proper spices for boiling the magic meat. This former wife was very tall, with beautiful but hard features—it was her self-reliant nature, perhaps, that gave her this mannish appearance. She lived with her family, but provided for herself by spinning wool and weaving cloaks and other garments, then sending these off to the market. She was the one, it was said, who'd demanded the divorce, giving as her grounds that she wanted to escape the beast before the beast ate her. She'd had a dream in which her husband wiped out all the gazelles in the Hamada, then came back home and, when he couldn't find any meat there, leaped on her and started tearing at her. She never stopped thanking God she'd borne him no children. She got her divorce from the judge with

Cain's agreement, but this hadn't turned her into an enemy; indeed their relations became warmer and more human, and she'd constantly be seen sending some lad to him with a pot of couscous, or bent by the well washing his clothes.

At the dinner he was confronted, to his great surprise, with the talismans. It wasn't just Masoud who came with one hanging around his neck. John too, as he squatted by the hearth, brought out a leather amulet marked with symbols made by the black magicians, waving it proudly in front of Cain. Cain took it and turned it over.

"These are the designs of those devils in Kano," he said. "These are their symbols, the lines they draw. How did an American Christian, living in the Naffousa mountain, come by a jinni amulet like this?"

The other two laughed. John winked, and Masoud, flinging wood onto the fire, said: "It's down to me. I took him to this black 'devil,' as you call him. The man had come along with the caravan. He made one like it for me." He opened his khaki shirt to reveal a piece of leather marked with similar magic symbols.

"Why didn't you tell me?" Cain shouted. "I didn't know you needed amulets when you had a dinner with *waddan!*"

"Everyone knows that," Masoud retorted. "Even the mountain children. The *waddan* has the spirit of the mountain in it. Anyone who eats it has to protect himself with an amulet. You don't play around with spirits. Do anything else, but not that."

He patted his amulet, then kissed it, before tucking it once more inside his shirt. "If John found out about it," he went on, "how come you didn't know?"

"And who let him into the secret, eh? Tell me that."

"I didn't tell him. I just took him to the soothsayer in the caravan."

"And who told him if you didn't?"

"Ask him."

John laughed. "Don't forget," he said, gazing at the steam rising up out of the pot. "I'm friendly with the Qadiri *shaykh*, the one you call a religious crank."

"You mean you're friends again?" Cain said.

"Well, no, he still won't make up with me. He's never forgiven me for killing all the gazelles. According to him, I don't belong to the religion of Jesus, and the religion of Jesus has nothing to do with me. He actually avoids me now."

Cain laughed.

"He's right," he said. "You're the biggest criminal who's ever come to this country. Who was it brought the Land Rover to the Hamada, and the bullets, and the flying Grasshoppers?"

"Well, you led the expeditions. Why did we do it all anyway? To calm down those worms in our leader's teeth!"

Their laughter rang through the desert.

"Oh," Masoud said, "if you'd only seen that fearsome soothsayer questioning John, you'd have died of laughter. He stared at him with his red eyes, then asked: 'What's your mother's name?' 'Isn't my father's name enough?' John said. 'That's for me to decide,' the magician said. 'Unless I know your mother's name, it's not going to work.' 'But my father's my father,' John insisted. The magician had had enough now. 'Your mother gave birth to you, didn't she?' he yelled. 'Whoever your father was.' I laughed at that, but the old man shut me up with a nasty look from those red eyes of his. 'You're all suspicious of Christian women,' John said. 'You think they're wanton and loose.' 'We're suspicious of every woman in this world,' the magician retorted. 'A woman's a woman, and the devil's her companion, whether she's from Kano or the isles of Waq Waq. And as for us soothsayers, we don't assume who anyone's father is, because we see things the way they are, without any illusions. Now, are you going to tell me your mother's name, or would you rather go ahead and eat charmed meat without an amulet?' So John gave in and told him his mother's name."

They shouted with laughter, the echo ringing once more through the silent, dark expanses. Then Cain returned to the matter in hand.

"So, it seems I'm the only one here who's going to eat *waddan* meat without an amulet."

Masoud set the pot firmly on the three-cornered stone hearth, then put more wood underneath.

"You've nothing to be afraid of," he said. "You were weaned on gazelle blood, weren't you? You're the spirit of the desert, and the *waddan*'s the spirit of the mountains. With God's help, one spirit's guarded against another."

Cain repeated the old rhyme: "'Oil from Gharyan. Dates from Fezzan. And meat? The *waddan*!' It doesn't say anything about gazelles."

A silence fell, and the darkness grew thicker still. Cain moved some of the blazing sticks and rolled aside some embers, on which he put the kettle to boil for tea. Masoud went on feeding the fire.

"I read about the secret of the gazelle," John said, "but I reckon that Sufi, whoever he was, didn't know everything. A few days back I went to the library at the base and looked up the *waddan* in the encyclopedia. Did you know the animal's been extinct since the seventeenth century?"

Masoud and Cain exchanged glances.

"The last *waddan*," John went on, gazing into the flames, "was apparently killed by a French prince in 1627. So how did it turn up in the Sahara?"

"Don't be too surprised," Masoud said. "Our desert hides all sorts of treasures, including extinct animals."

John watched the fire devouring the wood.

"So your soothsayers are right," he whispered, as if in a dream. "If there's a secret in an extinct animal, you really need amulets and spells."

John Parker wasn't John Parker that night. His voice borrowed the murmurs of the jinn in the heights, and took on the magical silence of the desert. So it was that he spoke like one of the priest sages.

25. THE VISION

Before that vision, Cain had never supposed the eyes of any animal could rival a gazelle's in expression, in magic and intelligence. Now, though, he saw eyes unmatched among all the animals, indeed among all the creatures of the world. The secret lay not in their beauty, as with the gazelle, but in their mystery. They said everything, even things no word could express. No speech was necessary.

After the dinner that Friday evening, Cain ate no meat for a whole week—Masoud hadn't managed to buy a lamb on credit. And so he'd taken to his bed, his head splitting, the worm gnawing at his teeth. He felt sick to the stomach.

Toward evening his fever would mount, and he vomited a number of times. Masoud visited him, bringing him fenugreek soup from his divorced wife, but, the moment he smelled no meat, he refused to touch it.

"It'll do you good," Masoud said. "It brings fever down."

But Cain thrust the plate away, repeating, as if in a trance: "The only thing that will cure me is meat. You know that well enough. My head's splitting. I can't take it any more."

It wasn't easy, in those years, to get hold of meat. The oasis people mostly slaughtered just at the Eid feast, though every so often they'd pool their money to buy a goat or a lamb, which would then be cut into small portions and divided among the families of those who'd contributed. In years when the heavens were merciful and plenty of rain fell, they might venture to slaughter a camel, and then those too poor to contribute in the normal way would be given a portion out of charity, as a kind of thanksgiving that the skies had relented.

In ordinary times, though, the poor could aspire to nothing from any slaughtered animal; and so they closed their doors tight, put out the fires in their hearths and kept their children shut up inside, so their appetites wouldn't be roused by the smell of meat cooking in other houses. And yet, for all these precautions, many people used to eating meat fell victim to the strange illness brought on by its lack.

It had never occurred to Cain, who'd eaten such huge amounts of meat, tickling his palate with the tastiest kinds, that one day the Hamada's teeming stock of gazelles would run out. He'd never supposed the fiercest hunter the desert had known would lie helpless in his bed, his head bursting for lack of meat.

Next day Masoud came from John's camp with cans of meat, tuna, and sardines, and a particular kind of red meat in a round pink box, which, according to John, was the meat of some kind of bird. But Cain threw up violently, and Masoud hovered around him through the night, before finally setting a gas lamp at the head of the bed and returning home.

And the moment he left, the *waddan* came to Cain. On his head were two huge horns curving to his back, then pointing up once more toward the head. In the dim light of the lamp, Cain saw the eyes. Were they whispering the secret of creation? Speaking of the fashioning of the desert, of the universe? Saying something of doomsday? Were they telling how he'd betrayed the gazelle, threatening some reprisal? He exchanged speech with those eyes, and roles too. He vanished in them and they in him, so that none could tell where he was or what he was. He was the *waddan*, and the *waddan* was Cain.

The mysterious animal invited him on a journey, and together they wandered, lost in the desert. He crossed the Hamada, riding on its back. He was thirsty and hungry, the ache was splitting his head. But now the *waddan* had borne him over the sandy waves, and there was another desert flooded with mirage, the sun's rays pouring down over its dunes. His headache, his thirst and hunger, grew ever fiercer, until he almost fell from the mighty beast's back. It had borne him to a mountainous desert now, its rugged slopes dotted with gloomy, open caverns and dark caves. The *waddan* moved with astounding grace among the merciless rocks. Cain was exhausted, but his worst affliction was hunger, the devilish worm moving within his teeth. He tore a piece of meat from the *waddan*'s neck and devoured it. But the beast leaped on among the mountain crags. He sank his teeth in the neck, chewed another piece of meat, then went on tearing the meat from the body, and still the beast sped on, his speed redoubled with every morsel Cain took, until his hooves left the ground altogether. They were flying, hanging in the air. The beast climbed to a high mountain peak, and Cain found he was sitting, now, on the back of a wretched man he didn't know, a tall, gaunt man whose neck dripped with blood. Before Cain woke from the horror of the transformation, the man raised his face of wretchedness toward him, and said: "Only through dust will the son of Adam be filled." Then the man flung him from the soaring peak, and he found himself plunging down into the pit.

ﻰﻠﺻ

26. THE BLEEDING OF THE STONE

Now at that time Libya was dry and bereft of moisture, and the band of nymphs, their hair unbound, bewailed its springs and lakes.
—Ovid, *Metamorphoses*

The sun sent down its twilight rays, so that Asouf couldn't open his eyes. The sun, after first rising, is always angry, arrogant, vengeful. Only with sunset does its fierceness begin to fade, as, overtaken by age, it kneels a humble supplicant before sinking toward its daily void.

He remembered how the crazed *waddan* had led him on, then flung him down into the pit, leaving him hanging at its mouth; and how, but for the great secret his father had bequeathed him, the gift of patience—the sole secret able to vanquish the desert—he would never have been delivered from his plight.

That dreadful thing, though, had happened in his youth. Now sheer weakness forced him to bow his head, to break in pieces on the rock as the proud sun does when it vanishes at its setting. But for old age, he would never have surrendered so quickly to the third condition. Before, at the pit, he'd resisted long before reaching this state, resisted until the wondrous *waddan* had plucked him out and he'd found himself tumbling down the slope. He was like the possessed waran now, which he'd slain in the morning and put in his bag, only to find it run off, dead though it was, when he'd flung it into the fire that evening. Here he was now, leaving life and yet not entering death. He was knocking on a door, between death and life.

Cain stood there, in front of the crucified body on the rock, beating his head with his two fists to lessen the sharp pain. A long thread of spittle, dripping from his mouth, glinted beneath the rays of the twilight sun, then fell to the ground. The south wind blew, and Cain's madness grew more raging.

"Speak up, you cursed old fool!" he shrieked. "Where have you hidden those animals?"

And the herdsman murmured his charm: "Only through dust will the son of Adam be filled."

He uttered this fainting, behind a door between earth and heaven, life and death.

Cain pounded his head once more, then shouted to Masoud.

"I remember now. I remember! This is the animal that came to me the other night. This is the devil that flung me down in the pit. How could I ever have forgotten? What made me want to come to this empty wilderness anyway? I remember! I was clutching on to this devil's horns." He laughed. "Look! Just look at his horns! Aren't they the horns of the accursed devil in the Quran?"

As he began laughing again, more spittle began to drip, in thin threads. And each time he broke into fresh shrieks of laughter, further shining threads would spew out. The sight turned Masoud sick. He'd never seen Cain in such a state.

Feeling a lurking anxiety now, he went up to his friend.

"That's enough," he said pleadingly. "That's enough now. It's time we left. We'll look for some meat in the nearest oasis. I'll find you some meat, I promise I will."

Cain thrashed out with his hand.

"Are you mad?" he shrieked. "Or is this your idea of a joke? We've crossed deserts, we've put up with hunger and thirst. And now we're supposed to go back to the oases, without any *waddan*? Go back there empty-handed? Get off! Get away from me!"

His eyes, sinking into their sockets, became fiercer and crueler. He moved toward the tent.

"Why don't you stop talking rubbish," he shouted, "and try to loosen this cursed wretch's tongue? Find out where he's hiding those *waddan* of his."

He rummaged among the crockery, then came back to the sandy area. His face was pale, the cheeks sunk deeper, and his eyes were bulging out. The odd light in his eyes left Masoud still more anxious than before. He saw the knife glittering in Cain's hand as he moved ever closer toward his victim. He ran to block the way.

"Cain!" he entreated. "What are you doing? The sun's got to you. Why don't we get away from here, now? I—"

He swallowed with difficulty, then fell on his knees in front of his friend.

"It's all right," he went on. "I know where he hides those animals of his. We'll go to Massak Mallat. It's less than a few miles from here."

Cain gave a crazy laugh.

"I don't need your animals now," he said, brandishing the glittering knife in the air. "I've my own sacrificial animal. Look! Do you see that *waddan* hanging there? It's a *waddan*.

Why didn't I see it earlier? What an utter fool I was!"

He struck his own head with the blade of the knife, and began to sway. Masoud got up and once more blocked the way, but Cain thrust him aside. He lost his balance and fell, then, getting up, tried to snatch the knife from Cain's hand, but Cain stabbed at him viciously, and Masoud only just swayed away in time, escaping with a wound on the wrist. Blood came spurting out, the drops falling onto the thirsty sand.

Cain stood there at Asouf's feet, where Asouf hung from the rocky face, his head dangling down on his breast, his face drained of color, his lips white and cracked from thirst and the south winds. His body was thrust into the hollow of the rock, merging with the body of the *waddan* painted there. The *waddan*'s horns were coiled around his own neck like a snake. The masked priest's hand still touched his shoulders, as if blessing him with secret rites.

Cain turned to climb the rock from its west side. Masoud yet again tried to block the way, stretching out his arms as if to embrace him.

"Curse the devil," he muttered, "and throw away that knife."

Cain waved the weapon menacingly in the air, and Masoud retreated. Then Cain climbed the rock from the flatter side, and, laughing wildly into the face of the sun, bent over the herdsman's head where it hung bowed. Taking hold of the beard, he passed the knife over Asouf's neck in the manner of one well used to slaughter, one who'd slaughtered all the herds of gazelles in the Red Hamada.

Asouf didn't shriek or make any protest. It was Masoud who screamed, the sound ringing through the nearby mountain peaks. The jinni maidens in the caves responded with their lamentations, and the mountain was rent. The face of the sun turned dark, and the banks of the wadi vanished in the eternal desert.

The murderer flung the head down on a flat stone there in front of the rock. Asouf's lips moved. The head, severed from the body, murmured: "Only through dust will the son of Adam be filled."

Blood dripped onto the surface of this stone half buried in the earth. On the stone, in the mysterious Touareg alphabet resembling the symbols of Kano soothsayers, was written the following:

> I, the High Priest of Matkhandoush, prophesy, for the generations to come, that redemption will be at hand when the sacred *waddan* bleeds and the blood issues from the stone. It is then that the miracle will be born; that the earth will be cleansed and the deluge cover the desert.

Still the blood poured over the surface of the stone buried in the lap of the sand. The murderer had no eyes to see how the sky had darkened, how clouds had blocked out the desert sun.

Masoud leaped into the truck and switched on the engine. At the same moment great drops of rain began to beat on its windows, washing away, too, the blood of the man crucified on the face of the rock.

NOTES

[i] The *Fatiha* is the short chapter that begins the Quran. It is recited by Muslims on every kind of important occasion: birth, engagement, marriage, death, the making of a contract, etc.

[ii] The *waddan*, or moufflon, a kind of wild mountain sheep, is the oldest animal in the Sahara. It became extinct in Europe as early as the seventeenth century.

[iii] The *qibla* is the direction of the Ka'aba, the sacred shrine within the Great Mosque in Mecca, to which Muslims turn during prayer.

[iv] *Zakat* is a tax obligatory on Muslims, the proceeds being used primarily for relief of the poor and needy. Prayer, payment of *zakat*, and the pilgrimage to Mecca are three of the five "pillars of Islam."

[v] *Muwwal*: A kind of traditional song, full of serious feeling. In this book, usually an elegiac song.

[vi] In the Muslim religion, animals whose meat is lawful to eat must be slaughtered alive. Dead animals are viewed as corpses, and eating their meat is unlawful.

[vii] A reference to the Italian invasion of Abyssinia, ordered by Mussolini in 1935.

[viii] *Dhikr*: Chant and ritual practiced by Sufi mystics.

[ix] The Hasawna Mountains are a range stretching south from the Red Hamada, separating this from the sandy desert in Fezzan.

Emerging Voices
New International Fiction Series
The best way to learn about people and places far away

This series is designed to bring to North American readers the once-unheard voices of writers who have achieved wide acclaim at home, but have not been recognized beyond the borders of their native lands. It publishes the best of the world's contemporary literature in translation and in original English.

Already published in the series

At the Wall of the Almighty by Farnoosh Moshiri (Iran) $16.00 pb
A Balcony Over the Fakihani by Liyana Badr (Palestine) $9.95 pb
Cages on Opposite Shores by Janset Berkok Shami (Turkey) $11.95 pb
The Children Who Sleep by the River by Debbie Taylor
   (Zimbabwe) $9.95 pb
The Dawning by Milka Bajic-Poderegin (Serbia) $14.95 pb
The Days of Miracles and Wonders by Simon Louvish (Israel) $16.00 pb
The End Play by Indira Mahindra (India) $11.95 pb
The Gardens of Light by Amin Maalouf (Lebanon) $15.00 pb
The Hostage by Zayd Mutee'Dammaj (Yemen) $10.95 pb
House of the Winds by Mia Yun (Korea) $22.95 hb
A Lake Beyond the Wind by Yahya Yakhlif (Palestine) $12.95 pb
Living, Loving and Lying Awake at Night by Sindiwe Magona
   (South Africa) $11.95 pb
Pillars of Salt by Fadia Faqir (Jordan) $12.95 pb
Prairies of Fever by Ibrahim Nasrallah (Jordan) $9.95 pb
Sabriya by Ulfat Idilbi (Syria) $12.95 pb
Samarkand by Amin Maalouf (Lebanon) $14.95 pb
The Secret Holy War of Santiago de Chile by Marco Antonio de la Parra
   (Chile) $12.95 pb
The Silencer by Simon Louvish (Israel) $10.95 pb
The Stone of Laughter by Hoda Barakat (Lebanon) $12.95 pb
Under the Silk Cotton Tree by Jean Buffong (Grenada) $9.95 pb
War in the Land of Egypt by Yusuf Al-Qa'id (Egypt) $12.95 pb
Wild Thorns by Sahar Khalifeh (Palestine) $12.95 pb

For a complete catalog please write to:
INTERLINK PUBLISHING
46 Crosby Street, Northampton, MA 01060
Tel: (413) 582-7054 Fax: (413) 582-7057 e-mail: info@interlinkbooks.com
website: www.interlinkbooks.com